The Companion

The Companion

a novel

Chaim Bermant

St. Martin's Press
New York

Library of Congress Cataloging-in-Publication Data

Bermant, Chaim.
    The companion.

    I. Title.
PR6052.E63C66   1988   823'.914   88-1935
ISBN 0-312-01751-0

First published in Great Britain by Robson Books Ltd.

First U.S. Edition

10 9 8 7 6 5 4 3 2 1

The Companion

1

I'VE FORGOTTEN HOW long we've been together but there's hardly a night when I ask myself why I don't do her in. I suppose it's because I'm too tired last thing at night, and by the time it gets to the morning I start thinking, it's a new day and things could start going right from now on, but of course they never do.

I suppose all this makes me sound like a disgruntled husband grumbling about his wife, but I'm not a husband and, if it comes to that, I'm not even married. I'm a companion.

I wasn't always a companion. I began as a maid, but when maids started getting decent wages and being called au-pairs and the like, she said she couldn't afford me, and began calling me her companion instead, and companions, as you know – or perhaps you don't – either aren't paid at all, or so little that it almost comes to the same thing. When I was her maid she ate in the dining room and I ate in the kitchen, but now that I'm her companion we both eat in the kitchen. The dining room she uses only at Christmas, or when we have company, which we almost never do.

In a way it's odd that she should want me of all people as her companion because, as she says often enough, she's sick of the sight of me, and hates me even more than I hate her, which is saying something, and if she could have opened her crippled fingers wide enough to handle a knife, she'd have stabbed me years ago.

Everybody tells me it's wrong to hate, but it can keep you warm on a cold night, and much as I hate her, I hate her dogs even more, small, smelly beasts like shaggy piglets, called Rigby and Digby. I give them a good kick when nobody's looking so that they take good care to keep out of my sight when she's out of the room.

Everybody calls her the Old Woman. Well she's old now, though she wasn't when I first started all those years ago, but the gardener called her the Old Woman, and it's been the Old Woman ever since. He's dead now, the gardener, but he stopped coming even before that because of what she was paying him, or rather, what she wasn't. I do the gardening now and in fact I don't mind it as long as she's not standing over me, or rather sitting over me, because she's grown to such a size that her legs can hardly take her and she spends most of her time in a wheelchair. You've heard of green fingers, and gold fingers? Well, I'm black fingers or at least that's what she calls me because she says nothing I touch grows, but things would grow all right if she wouldn't go breathing her poison all over them. I was pushing her in the park once when a whole line of chrysanths keeled over just as she was passing.

Her actual name is Crystal, Mrs Crystal, but if there ever was a Mr Crystal I've never set eyes on him, though she mentions him often enough, 'my late husband' this, and 'my late husband' that. He certainly wasn't around by the time I came, which, as I said, wasn't yesterday. I suppose he died young which, being married to her, must have been a mercy.

Her family, she kept telling me, were 'once people of consequence in the county, and even beyond', and she showed me a family tree which I couldn't follow (and which I don't think she could either) which, she said, showed that she was distantly related to Winston Churchill. When Harold Macmillan became Prime Minister, she said that she was also distantly related to him, 'through his wife's side naturally – she was a Cavendish. His own family were Scottish peasants.' She disliked Scotsmen, Welshmen, Irishmen, Jews, Catholics, blacks, foreigners in general and French foreigners in particular ('they are not to be trusted'). In fact she didn't much care for anyone and, if it came to that, no one much cared for her, except her dogs and Coggeshall, her solicitor.

She has a sister with whom she is not on speaking terms, though they used to be on writing terms, and they'd quarrel by

8

post, but that stopped since the price of stamps went up. She wants to outlive her sister, that's what keeps her going, and she will too. She'll outlive everybody. She sometimes has a moment of kindness – about once a year – and she'd point to this or that bit of junk (which I wouldn't use as a door-stop) and say, 'this'll be yours when I'm gone.' When she's gone? She'll outlive the devil himself.

If she should ever go, and, as I said, I can't see it happening (unless she's pushed) she'll probably leave everything to Coggeshall, her solicitor, a large, red-faced man with wavy hair, huge under-chin and thick glasses. He comes every three or four months and she has her hair done for him, and shaves the little beard on the point of her chin, and drenches herself with perfume, and large though he is he has those dainty little feet, and he almost comes dancing in with 'and how is my lovely?' and pinches her cheek and pats her knee and kisses her hand as if she's the Queen Mother, though how he can put that claw of hers to his lips, I can't tell. And I wouldn't like to think what else he does, for I always have to leave the room the minute he's there. For an afternoon or so afterward she's a new woman.

I used to think that Coggeshall was a suitor until I met Mrs Coggeshall, a very tall, very thin woman, whose veins stood out on her neck like ivy creepers on an old building. A few years after I joined the Old Woman, they made a birthday party for her. She didn't like to say which birthday. She looked too well-preserved to be eighty, and too far gone to be sixty, so it must have been seventy.

Coggeshall used to come down from London four times a year, and his clerk, Stanley, came about once a month. Stanley was an elderly, stooping figure, with white hair, who looked like Old Father Time, and if she was nearly always cheered by Coggeshall, she was nearly always depressed by Stanley. Well, the sight of old Stanley was enough to depress anyone, but I think what happened was that Coggeshall brought money and Stanley brought bills.

Coggeshall, of course, was always entertained in the drawing-room, while she left me to entertain Stanley in the kitchen. He would have tea and toast and would sometimes vary it by having toast and tea. I once offered to make him an omelette, and he said 'that is very kind of you, but I'm afraid I can't take exotic food. You see I have this ulcer.' He didn't actually show me his ulcer, but if it wasn't for his ulcer we would have had nothing to talk about. I sometimes tried to draw him out about Coggeshall and the Old Woman, but either he didn't know, or wouldn't be drawn, though he once did go as far as to say that the Old Woman could be difficult.

'Difficult?' I said, 'Have you ever known her to be easy?'

'Well, people do get like that when they get on,' he said.

'That's because they're never told where to get off,' I said. 'You spoil her, that's what you do. "Yes, Mrs Crystal. Certainly, Mrs Crystal. Absolutely, Mrs Crystal." I mean it's not even as if she's got any money – or at least she says she hasn't.'

I waited to see if he might contradict me one way or the other. He allowed something like a smile to lighten up his watery eyes, but, as always, he kept his mouth shut.

When the gardener was still alive he told me that the Old Woman used to have a 'fancy man'. He didn't live long enough to tell me what he meant by that, and I suppose by the time I joined her she was too old to need one.

Yet she was never too old for Coggeshall and, for all her huge bulk and crippled joints, she became playful and coquettish, and all through lunch there was such a traffic of little signals between them that I felt out of place.

She must have been not bad looking once, to judge from the photos she has around, some framed, some stuck in the corners of larger pictures and curling at the corners, some under the glass top of her dresser, all fading. There are also photos of men in uniform and girls in party frocks. She keeps talking about her coming-out party and how she was presented to the Queen. She doesn't say which Queen. It could have been Victoria.

'My mother was a Poster, you know,' she said to me once, as if that should mean anything to me. 'A bill-poster or a four poster?' I asked.

'Looking at me now, you wouldn't think I was once one of the most sought-after young women in the country,' she said. As a matter of fact I did, but I wouldn't give her the pleasure of saying so, and I said instead: 'What's happened to you since?'

Her father, a brigadier, was killed in the First World War. Her husband died in the Second. 'He wasn't even killed,' she would say, as if dying a natural death was a dishonourable way to go. He caught pneumonia and that was it. She herself was an officer in the WAAFS and had caught something or other in India which had left her an invalid.

'It's not easy to be what I am when I think of what I was,' she kept telling me, as if to say – 'It's all right for you, seeing you were never anything in the first place.

As a matter of fact I come from a pretty good family myself, or at least, a pretty respectable one. My father was a station master with the Great Western Railway. It wasn't a large station, in fact I don't think more than two trains passed through it on any one day, but it had a beautiful garden and father won prizes year after year for his dahlias and chrysanths. Then came the war – the Second one, I mean – and it was the end of his lovely dahlias and chrysanths, to say nothing of his roses and lupins. People used to say it was a pleasure to miss a train at dad's station, the flower beds were so lovely, but they all had to go so he planted cabbages and brussel-sprouts instead, but they never really took because his heart wasn't really in it. 'A flower man is a flower man and a vegetable man is a vegetable man,' he said, and he was a flower man. Besides, he didn't have time. Trains began roaring through the station at all times of the day and most times of the night, troop trains, freight trains, tanker trains. In the old days you could pick mushrooms between the tracks, now it was like Clapham Junction. Father's hearing had been damaged in the First war – one day he was crossing the line just as a train was coming and that was that. Mother took to her bed and never came down again.

There were three of us in the family, Arthur, Doris and myself. Doris was 'the pretty one', as mother and everyone

11

else called her, I wasn't. She was also the brainy one, which I wasn't either. When the war came she joined the Women's Land Army and one day she scratched herself on a rose bush. It wasn't even a bad scratch, but it became septic and within a month she was dead.

'Imagine *her* going', said mother resentfully, meaning, why couldn't it have been me. Dad said nothing at all. He stopped speaking from the day she died and was killed a week or two later on the line.

I looked after mother for fourteen years, but she wasn't an easy person to look after because, apart from anything else, although she had been slight in build (like myself) she grew to be as large and as heavy as the bed. It was a double bed with cast iron frame, and I half thought of fixing up a block and tackle every time I had to move her, because at first she didn't like to move and, by the time she died, she couldn't.

'I should never have married your father,' she kept saying over and over again.

'Why not?' I said, 'he was a nice enough man.'

'He was a hard-working man and good with flowers, but that isn't everything. Mother was against the marriage; "it'll come to no good", she kept telling me, "he's not our class", and he wasn't, but it was just after the war and nearly everyone I knew had been killed. You had to take what you could get.'

'The trouble with your father was that he was too contented. You put him anywhere and there he stopped. And he was an educated man too, or at least well-read. I mean he didn't go to university, but he read a lot, all the time. You could hardly talk to him because he was always bent over a book, but they didn't do much for him, his books or his reading. Flowers and books, books and flowers, and people promoted over him, right and left, men younger than him, and without his education, or family connections, but it didn't worry him a bit. As long as his flowers were blooming, he was happy. He spent more time on his flowers than his children. My father had a large business with twelve men on his staff, but we saw more of him than you saw of your father, *and* we had a nanny.'

Her father had owned a large drapery shop in Exeter where

they had been fairly well off. As she grew older she forgot that she was the widow of a railwayman and thought that she was still the daughter of a draper, and kept asking me to cook saddle of lamb and sirloin of beef as if money was no object.

In a way she was right about father neglecting his children. I can't remember being neglected myself, but then I can't remember being a child because even when I was at school I had to rush home to go on this or that errand because we lived a good bit away from the village, and mother didn't always have time to get to the shops, but I do remember my brother, Arthur, falling into bad company and getting into trouble. It all started when a branch of Woolworths opened in the next town and he used to come back on Saturday afternoons with pockets bulging with marbles, pencils, rubbers, chocolates, toothpaste, soap, boot laces, boot polish, bird seed, bath salts, mouse traps, corn plasters, buttons, thimbles, sewing thread, ribbons, safety pins, cough mixture, hair oil, egg whisks, sanitary napkins, denture powders, nail files, nail varnish, vanishing cream, lip stick, perfumes, so that by the time they caught him he was ready to open his own shop.

When the war broke out he faked his age (he was only sixteen) and joined the army, and was taken prisoner (though if you ask me, he deserted) during the fighting in Egypt. I wasn't too sure what he did after the war, and I was half afraid to ask, for he would pop up from nowhere in the middle of the night. Sometimes he would have money, and he'd give me five or even ten pounds and tell me to buy myself something nice, but more often he didn't, and he'd stay around for a few days, or even a few weeks, picking his nose and eating us out of house and home. He'd never show his face outside, not in broad daylight, and would dive into the garden shed everytime there was a knock at the door.

Once he turned up with a woman. I took one look at her and said:

'She is not coming in here, this is a respectable house.'

'But look at the weather', he said, 'It's raining down in buckets.'

'I don't care about the weather, she's not coming in here.'

After they talked it over for a bit she went out into the rain and he came into the house. Not very gallant my brother.

An hour or two later I got up to go to the bathroom but, when I tried the handle, it was locked. I went to the downstairs, and it was locked as well, so I went back upstairs, and it was only then that it occured to me that since mother was in bed and I was on the landing Arthur couldn't be occupying both the bathroom and toilet at the same time. He must have smuggled the trollop in. So I picked up a broom and waited in the dark, and as soon as she came out of the bathroom I whacked her across the head. I don't know if I really hurt her, but she got the fright of her life and went screaming down the stairs. Arthur came out of the toilet at that moment holding his trousers up with his hand. She ran past him out into the street, and he went running after her, tripping over his trousers.

In the meantime mother had been wakened by the commotion and was sitting up in bed in hysterics, and it took the doctor and half a bottle of pills to calm her down.

That was the last I saw of Arthur for a while. Perhaps I had been a bit hard on him – and her – but as it was I had to spend the better part of the day disinfecting every inch of the bathroom and the spare bedroom and, for good measure, the downstairs toilet.

Mother, by this time, lived on pills. She took pills to get to sleep, and pills to stay awake, pills before meals and pills after meals and sometimes even pills during meals, though they didn't seem to do her much good, especially as about half of them were taken to offset the side effects of the other half.

One day, the family doctor, a sad little man with a wrinkled neck who looked like a tortoise who'd been winkled out of his shell, suggested that she should be moved into hospital.

'What good would that do?' I asked.

'It would give you a break,' he said.

Up to then it hadn't occured to me that I needed a break.

'What time do you start your day?' he asked.

'I don't know. I get up when she calls me. We hardly use a clock in this house.'

'I'll take her into hospital and you have a break,' he said, 'because if you don't ease off, you'll have to be going in yourself.' He 'phoned the hospital there and then. I don't know if she heard him but when they came to fetch her, she was dead.

He was a nice man, the doctor, but he didn't know what he was talking about, at least about me needing a break, because I had a long break after that and the first thing that happened was that I had a breakdown and had to go into hospital after all.

Mother had left half her money to the Distressed Gentlefolk Aid Society and half to me, but in fact nearly all her money was gone. There was only the house, and that belonged to the railway company, and by the time I had paid for the funeral and other expenses, there was only about fifty pounds left.

When I was ill in hospital, I was visited by the vicar who asked me what I planned to do with myself. I didn't really know because I had never made plans in my life and, besides, I had no training or anything like that. I had done nothing except look after mother.

'But that's an invaluable experience in itself,' he said. 'There's many a poor woman who is in need of the sort of succour you brought to your dear parent.' When I came out he introduced me to the Old Woman, and I've been with her since. I wouldn't say I bless the day I met her, and in fact it's half turned me off Christianity.

2

WE HAD LIVED on the edge of a village. The Old Woman lived in a large town called Crumpshall. Mother was always hoping that father might one day become station master of Crumpshall and, had he lived, he might have made it.

When I was small, before the war, we used to be taken for our Christmas treats to Crumpshall. We would do our Christmas shopping at Crossleys, the local Harrods, and would be taken to the pantomime at the Crumpshall Pavilion, and I still remember the dress and shoes I wore when we were taken to something grand at the Pump Rooms to celebrate the Silver Jubilee in 1935. The Old Woman lived in a large, yellow-brick house at the end of a long crescent of large houses, not far from the Pump Rooms. The whole crescent must have been very grand in its day but, by the time I came, most of the houses had been converted into offices, or shabby little hotels, and only two were still used as private homes – 'Eden', where the Old Woman lived, and 'Halcyon', which was the home of Mrs Kilpatrick.

Mrs Kilpatrick must have been a giant at one time for, although she was nearly bent double, she was still taller than either the Old Woman or me.

The Old Woman and Mrs Kilpatrick, Martha and Veronica, were on first-name terms and would visit each other twice a week, for tea. We would go to her on Tuesdays and she would come to us on Thursdays. Both would bring out silver tea-pots and serve Earl Grey tea with cucumber sandwiches and Fuller's walnut cake which they bought in Crossleys. They both had accounts in Crossleys, and would do their weekly shopping about the same time, except before Christmas, when they would share a hired car and go up to London.

The Old Woman used to have her own car and chauffeur. 'A Daimler', she said, 'it was like a travelling drawing room. The driver was behind a soundproof partition. One spoke to him through a tube and one could conduct a private conversation without any distraction. We travelled right across France after we married, then along the Riviera and into Italy. One didn't have to be rich to travel in style in those days. There were children around who didn't know what the sea was and in the summer I would have Ritchie take them on a run to Brighton or Southend. The car was large and they were skinny, so he could take a dozen at a time. Nowadays, of course, they all go to Majorca and Minorca, and the Costa del this and the Costa del that, and I hardly go anywhere.'

She sold the car after the war to Ritchie, who started up his own car-hire company, and she still treated him as if he was her chauffeur and he, for his part, liked to pretend that he was. He also charged much less than anyone else, but he and his car had both got on in years, and hiring him was always something of an adventure for you were never sure when you were going to get there, or even if you were going to get there.

Ritchie told me a few things about the Old Woman's husband, Edgar, which he thought she didn't know.

'Oh, he was once for the ladies, and he liked them big, though he was small himself, little bantam cock of a man, but he'd have two or three of them at the back there.'

'At the same time?'

'At the same time. And the things that went on. Every time I looked into the driving mirror I nearly went off the road. And first thing in the morning too, that was the funny thing. She thought I was taking him to the station, but I wasn't. Two or three of them at a time, four sometimes. It's a miracle the springs could take it.' By the look of his car, they couldn't.

He also knew Veronica's husband, Mr Kilpatrick.

'Very tall, very quiet, never said anything, always in black. He always looked as if he was on the way to a funeral, or coming from one.' He was in fact the secretary of a large company, but I suppose being married to Veronica was as good as a funeral.

17

I don't know if Veronica was the Old Woman's best friend, though she was the friend she saw most often, but she was very scathing about her.

'Rotten with money . . . Her father made it in the war, you know, the first one, when it was easy to make . . . She's half Irish . . . Can never keep a servant.'

The servant she did have about the time I came was a plump, breathless woman with thick glasses, called Emily, who was also a 'companion', probably for the same reasons as me. Emily was my best friend, in fact my only friend, at least in Crumpshall. It wasn't difficult to make her cry and her sobbing sometimes got on my nerves, but she did have to work rather hard for her keep. Although the Old Woman liked to have her wheelchair around, she sometimes managed on her sticks for whole days at a time, whereas Veronica could hardly manage more than five yards on her feet, and Emily had to push her everywhere. She must have weighed about a ton, so pushing her at all was a job, and it was worse in Crumpshall, which is all hills, and I don't know how Emily managed to stay as plump as she was. Perhaps she grew fat on religion. She spent most of her free time in church, which didn't bother me too much, but when she was perky – which thank God wasn't often – she would burst into hymns, which could be embarrassing. She also had a weakness for vicars and curates and vergers, partly, I suppose, because they were about the only men she came across. The family had been deserted by their father before she was born, and she had two older sisters. She had gone to a girl's school and during the war had worked in a parachute factory, which was full of women.

'The things they *said*, and the things they *did*, Phyllis, you can't imagine.'

'But if there were only women about, who did they do it with?'

'I don't know, they always found somebody. They were shameless.'

She was very proper, Emily, and had a weakness for hats. In fact she spent nearly everything she earned on hats, hats and the church poor box, though there couldn't have been many people in Crumpshall much poorer than her. It wasn't only that she was paid badly, she was treated badly.

The Dragon, as I called Veronica, couldn't open her mouth without breathing fire and brimstone and she'd reduce poor Emily to a quivering jelly, sometimes even in front of strangers.

I was with her once when the Dragon pointed to her hat and said:

'Where are you going?'

'Nowhere, Mrs Kilpatrick.'

'Then why are you wearing that hat?'

'I've just been to church.'

'You never told me you were going to church.'

'But I go every Sunday and you said I could.'

'You didn't tell me you were going this morning, you could have told me as a courtesy.'

'But you were still asleep.'

'I was not. I hardly ever sleep. I was just resting. You spend far too much time in church for your own good or anybody else's. I don't pay you to go to church. Goodness knows why I do pay you. Now take off that ridiculous hat and rub my back.'

'Why don't you answer back?' I kept saying to Emily.

'But Phyllis, how can I?' All she did was to rush upstairs to her tiny cupboard of a room, sit on her bed (it didn't have room for a chair) and weep.

It was the size of that room which got me because 'Halcyon' was even bigger than 'Eden', with larger rooms and more of them, but all she could spare for poor Emily was that little cupboard. Not that Emily ever complained.

'It's cosy,' she said, 'and easy to keep warm,' but then if you had put Emily in a hole in the ground, she would have said: 'Oh but it's lovely, it takes me right back to nature.'

We had five rooms upstairs and three downstairs, most of which were empty most of the time. Once, when I asked the Old Woman why she needed all those rooms, she said: 'You people who've been brought up in little cubicles don't understand the importance of space.' She used to have people coming to stay with her and I suppose she hoped that, for as long as she had the rooms, they might come again. Her hands

19

were crippled, but she managed to hold a pen between her fingers in the way men hold a cigar, and she had friends all over the world she would write to. They wrote back about once a year, around Christmas, and she would have all their Christmas cards strung out on a cord along her mantelpiece. The first year I came I counted sixty-six, but they got fewer and fewer until most of them from tradesmen like Lamb's, the butcher, and Pink, the ironmonger, and Crossleys, the department store, and she spaced them out more widely to make them look like many.

'Halcyon', from the outside, looked more or less like 'Eden', only you came in to a grand hall, with panelled walls and a grand staircase leading to a gallery, and the place was full of stuffed animals in glass cases and stuffed fish and mounted heads, most of them moth eaten. The Dragon's brother had been something important in Africa and had left her most of his trophies.

None of us knew what happened to Mr Kilpatrick. She once said she'd had a 'terrible war', and I thought she'd meant that he'd been killed in the fighting, but it was nothing like that. She'd had evacuees billeted on her from the East End of London and she sometimes woke screaming in the night dreaming that they were back. 'Dirt everywhere, noise all the time, and they'd steal things, and break things. I could have taken the bombing, but I couldn't take them. It was terrible, terrible.'

The Old Woman said that Mr Kilpatrick had vanished in the war. 'He'd been something important, with lots of pips on his shoulders, and if I remember rightly, even tabs on his lapels. One day he was reported missing and that was that, I don't know how though, for he wasn't in the front line and as far as I know he wasn't killed. Some people said he'd been seen in America, some in Australia, some in France, some even here in England, but Veronica never set eyes on him again, that's for sure. She keeps complaining about the measly pension she gets, as if she needs it. I'm not even sure she's entitled to it in the first place.'

Unlike the Old Woman, the Dragon sometimes had visitors, all of them long in the tooth, and all rather tall and fierce-looking. She usually had one or two guests over Christmas, and would always ask us over for Christmas dinner.

It was, I suppose, our great day of the year, and the Old Woman would put on her pearl necklace, a long, black velvet dress with a lace collar. But she couldn't use the wheelchair when she was in that dress because the train would get caught up in the wheels, so she'd have Ritchie drive her over.

The Dragon also had her Christmas cards strung out on a cord and when no one was looking, the Old Woman would count them to see if she had as many as her: she never did.

There would be a fire blazing in the hearth, and a Christmas tree with fairy lights and nicely packaged presents (the packages were nicer than the presents) and there was always plenty to eat and drink. The Dragon would be at the top of the table, with the Old Woman on one side and her guests on the other, and Emily and me down at the bottom, but what spoilt it for me was Emily jumping up and down as if she was on a spring. More often than not the Dragon wanted something or other, but even when she didn't, Emily still could not relax and I almost had to hold her down in her chair.

The talk was all about people with silly nick-names, like 'Pluto' and 'Jumbo' and 'Piggy', whom I'd never heard of. The Dragon, the guests, and the Old Woman had glass after glass of wine, but the bottles stayed at the top end of the table. Once I asked them to be passed down. Although the conversation stopped for a moment she did as I asked, but the Old Woman said to me later: 'If you're going to embarrass me like that in public again, I shan't take you with me.' I didn't promise to behave, and it wouldn't have helped if I had because, although neither of us knew it, there wouldn't be an again.

The Old Woman used to go to church fairly regularly, but after the old vicar moved on (he didn't die, vicars never do), she stopped going because she didn't care for the new one. He was a fresh faced young man with pink cheeks and a jolly manner, but she didn't like to be jollied. She didn't like his accent either or his sermons, or his wife ('She wears trousers. Can you imagine it? The vicar's wife in trousers!') and instead of church, we would have a walk in the park, though if the

21

weather was bad I'd go to church with Emily (not for Christ's sake but for Emily's sake). Emily loved the vicar, and his accent and his sermons, though she wasn't all that much taken with the wife, who was a thin thing with a white face, hollow chest and large glasses.

One day after the service – to this day I don't know what made me think of it, perhaps I wanted her to try something daring – I asked Emily if she would like to go into a pub.

'A pub? Oh, I couldn't do that.'

'Why not?'

'I've never done it before.'

'That's all the more reason why you should do it now.'

'Isn't it expensive?'

'Not if you only have a glass of beer or lemonade.'

And I almost had to drag her in, but once inside she quite enjoyed it and felt rather pleased with herself for being so daring. We had been there for about ten minutes when a man with a red face, a cigarette in his mouth and a battered hat on his head, came over and sat down beside Emily, and, without a word of introduction, said to her:

'Are you from here?' She looked at me wondering what to do next.

'Answer the gentleman,' I said.

'Yes,' she said.

'I've never seen you here before.'

'Oh I've never been here before.'

'That accounts for it, doesn't it? Will you have a drink?'

'I've got one, thank you.'

'Have another.'

She looked at me again.

'Do you want another?' I asked.

'No, not really.'

'She doesn't,' I said, 'but I do.'

And he looked at me as if he'd noticed me for the first time, which perhaps he had, for he screwed up his eyes as if he hadn't quite taken me in.

'Did you say you wanted another?'

'A Guinness,' I said.

And he looked at me again and got up to get one.

'He fancies you,' I said to Emily.

'Go on.'

'He does.'

And he did, though for the life of me I couldn't see why, perhaps because there was quite a bit of her. In a way I was upset, not because he didn't fancy me, for I didn't fancy him, but because it reminded me of the times Doris and me went out together. No one had an eye for me, but Doris was good looking. Not to be noticed with Emily was another matter and when I got home I sat down and had a long, hard look at myself in the mirror. I couldn't have called myself a beauty – neither, for that matter, would anyone else, but I was just over fifty, and didn't look more than my age, and I wasn't ugly, or at least, I thought I wasn't. My hair was rather straight and beginning to go grey, and I wore glasses, but they weren't thick glasses like Emily's. I was slight compared to her, which I hadn't thought was a bad thing, but men like a bit of meat, I suppose, and I didn't have much of it. It was the chest, I suppose, which counted. I was a bit flat, whereas Emily stood out nicely at the front. (She also stood out nicely at the back, but it was the front which mattered.)

The man, who was called Horace, was a farmer. His mother had died recently and he had decided to get married.

'There's nothing much where I come from, that's why I come here every Sunday.' He lived in a small village about ten miles away. He drove us home in a very old car which smelt of poultry and burning rubber. When he dropped us off he said to Emily:

'Shall I see you next Sunday then?'

'If you like.'

'In the pub?'

'If you like.'

'At the same time?'

'All right.'

For the rest of that week she was in a daze and nearly pushed the Dragon under a bus. ('You needn't have worried,' I told her, 'the bus would have got the worst of it.')

23

On Sunday morning she asked me to go to the pub with her.

'No, no,' I said, 'I'd cramp his style and yours. You're old enough to manage on your own.'

'But I can't go into the pub on my own.'

'He'll be there.'

'But supposing he's not?'

'Then you can come right out again.'

But he was there, and as soon as he'd bought her a lemonade he proposed. Who says farmers are slow?

She was drinking her lemonade at the time, and nearly choked.

'I hope you accepted,' I said.

'I couldn't, not just like that. I hardly know him, and then what would Mrs Kilpatrick say?'

'Mrs Kilpatrick! The first thing you want to do now is tell her to go to hell. What do you care about Mrs Kilpatrick?'

'You're not being serious now, Phyllis. I told him I would think about it.'

'When will you be seeing him next?'

'Sunday, he's taking me to see his farm. I hope you'll come with me. I daren't go alone.'

'Why not?'

'You know very well why not.'

I was afraid that if I didn't go the match would be off, but the Old Woman had expected me to go out with her, and I told her what had happened.

'Emily,' she said, 'Veronica's Emily?'

'Why not?'

'What could anyone possibly see in her?'

'That's not for me to say.'

'Has she told Veronica yet?'

'No, not yet, and don't you tell her either.'

'Veronica won't like it.'

'Veronica will have to lump it.'

That Sunday he drove us over to the farm and I hoped, as we rattled along, that his house was in better condition than his car. It wasn't. I was prepared for the worst, but Emily wasn't, and she looked around her with her hands to her cheeks. There was another surprise waiting for her when we went upstairs and found a dirty, shrivelled, old man under a heap of blankets.

'That's dad,' he said. 'He hasn't been himself since ma died, though he's harmless.' But at least the farm was in good shape, and he did have about eighty acres of land.

'I have a boy coming in to help out on the farm,' he said, 'but it's difficult to get help in the house, especially with the old man about. He frightens 'em, though he's harmless really.'

Emily wanted another week to make up her mind.

'I know what you're thinking,' I said, 'the place is a bit untidy and could do with a woman's hand, but it shouldn't take too long to put it right.'

'It wasn't the place I was thinking about at all. He is a bit common, you know.' I couldn't believe my ears.

'Common!'

'Well he's not what you'd call a gentleman farmer, is he?' I felt like saying: 'And who the hell do you think you are? A bleeding duchess?' I had always known she was dim and wet, but it hadn't occured to me she was downright stupid. I wanted to hit her.

'He's a decent, honest, hard working man and comfortable too. What the hell are you waiting for, a belted Earl?'

'I hope you won't think I'm a snob, Phyllis, but except when I worked in the parachute factory – and that was during the war – I've always been used to mixing with a better class of people.'

'What class of person do you think I am?' She had to think about that.

'Well I wouldn't call you common.'

'Thanks very much, but I'd marry him tomorrow if he asked me,' which, I think, helped her make up her mind and she accepted.

She now had to face the Dragon.

'I don't know what you've got to be afraid of. You're a free woman. You can walk out any time you like.'

'She might be upset.'

'I'm sure she will be. She'll not get herself another willing slave so easily, but that's her hard luck.'

The following Sunday Horace gave her a ring, with the tiniest diamond – it was like a grain of sugar – I had ever seen.

'That's made it easier for you,' I said. 'She'll ask you about the ring, you can tell her, and that'll be that.'

She asked her about the ring, but she couldn't quite bring herself to tell her straight out.

'It's . . . it's a present,' said Emily.

'A present? Is it your birthday?'

'No, not really.'

'What do you mean "not really". It either is, or it isn't.'

'It isn't.'

'What sort of present is it then?'

'An . . . engagement present.'

'A *what* present?'

'An engagement present.'

'An engagement present?'

I don't know how long the conversation went on, but later in the evening the Dragon 'phoned up the Old Woman and told her she was worried about Emily. 'The poor demented creature thinks she's about to get married.'

All three of us had to work on her before she realized that Emily was not imagining things, and when she did, she said:

'I'm not having it, that's all. I shan't allow it.' And what did Emily do next? She went up to her little cupboard and cried. I nearly cried myself when she told me.

They had arranged to marry in another four weeks.

'Look,' I said, 'write the Dragon a letter that you're leaving, and when the four weeks are up, leave.' She wrote the letter but one week passed, and then another, and the Dragon made no attempt to find a replacement and in fact did not even mention the letter.

'What am I going to do?' wailed Emily. 'What am I going to do? She can't be left on her own just like that.'

'Yes she can, if she wants to be.'

When a third week passed and she had still not found a replacement, Emily said: 'I can't leave her, I just can't,' and it was only then that it occured to me that she didn't really want to get married. She didn't come from a marrying family. Her

26

two sisters hadn't marrried, and I wasn't all that sure that her mother had. She was probably afraid of marriage. She didn't know what a man was and was afraid to find out. She had been dragging her feet from the moment Horace proposed, and I said to her: 'All right then, stay with the Dragon, but you'd better tell poor Horace you're wasting his time.'

'You're wrong,' she said, 'I'm very fond of Horace, he's a good man and I do want to get married.'

'But you don't want to leave the Dragon. All right, marry Horace and take the Dragon in with you. Perhaps she could marry his dad!'

'You're not being serious, are you Phyllis? I can never tell with you.'

Three days before the wedding she was still dithering, but then came a reprieve. Horace's father died and they had to postpone the wedding which she, for some reason, took as an omen. She didn't say 'no' for that would have upset Horace, but she wanted even more time to think about it, and while she was thinking about it, Horace also thought about it and found someone else (once his father was out of the way it wasn't difficult).

I thought the poor woman might go to pieces, but she came rushing over to me with the news as if it was the best thing that had happened since the resurrection. And I suppose it must have been a relief. She didn't have to make a decision, or face changes. Life would go on for the next twenty years as it had done for the last twenty. She could breathe again.

I was sorry it had all come to an end, and I wasn't. She was stupid and wet, but she was company, someone to go out with the odd moments we had to go out, and someone to talk to. I don't know what sort of companion the Dragon would have found in her place, or even if she would have found a companion at all, and I too wasn't keen on changes, but it would have been nice to go to a wedding. They make a change from funerals.

3

WE HAD MANY calendars in the house because when the Old Woman got a new one, she was too mean to throw out the old ones, and she liked to sit up in bed with her calendars round her to plan the year ahead, as if she was so busy, with so many calls on her time, that she had to have every minute organized.

Her year began in December. On the first Sunday she'd make out a list of people she'd send Christmas presents to and on the first Monday we'd travel to London with Emily and the Dragon. I'm not sure why they had to go to London. They never came back with anything they couldn't have bought in Crumpshall, and probably at half the price.

'When I was a young woman we used to go into London at least once a month, for the theatre, meals, shopping, parties,' said the Old Woman, 'and we were sometimes more in London than Crumpshall,' and I suppose they wanted to show their face in the capital at least once a year to show that they were not stuck out in the sticks for good. They would also show their face at church at least once a year to show that they were still fully paid-up Christians. It was an effort and expense, but it was the sort of effort and expense expected of people of their class.

She didn't have a long shopping list, and it grew shorter year by year, because half the people she knew she'd quarrelled with, and the other half were dead, which was perhaps just as well for she'd almost pass out when she discovered the price of things.

'But how can a single linen handkerchief cost that much?'

'I'm sorry, madam, I don't fix the prices.'

'I'll have the cotton ones instead.'

And it was the same in every department. I began to hate Christmas, even though she would always include some 'little surprise' for me among the gifts. Little it was, surprise it wasn't. In fact it was always the same thing, a bottle of Guinness wrapped up in fancy paper. She once saw me having a glass of the stuff in the kitchen, and ever since she had a habit of wagging a crippled finger at me and saying: 'I know your little secret, don't I?' as if I was a chronic alcoholic. Then she would buy perfume for the Dragon, a pocket diary for Emily and an ounce of pipe tobacco for old Ritchie. I don't know if Ritchie smoked, and he certainly never smoked a pipe, but she once said that you could always trust a man with a pipe and I suppose that by giving him pipe tobacco she thought he could be relied on, which he could, even if his car couldn't. Other presents were for distant relatives I had never met, including a Lady something or other, and I half think they were names she'd made up to convince herself she wasn't alone in the world.

'When I was a girl the presents would arrive by the van-load,' she said. 'The house was full of guests. They would arrive towards the end of December and stay until about the middle of January. Grandmother had a very big house, a huge garden, a park really, with a pond. Winters must have been very much colder than they are now, for the pond always seemed to be frozen over and we would go skating and then as the skies reddened and darkness fell, we'd go home to tea before a blazing log fire – muffins, crumpets, tea-cakes, all toasted and steaming, with melting butter and thick raspberry jam. There would be twenty to thirty of us around the Christmas table, sometimes more, and we'd have visitors from India and Malaya and Singapore, and what marvellous stories they would tell. And the women looked so grand in their satin dresses with the leg of mutton sleeves, and there was Monck, the butler, a very imposing figure. Grandfather had been a general, but Monck was in command, and then there was Uncle Edward – the explorer who brought us all presents made out of shark's teeth – and Uncle Herbert, the suffragan bishop. Such magnificent figures.'

'What happened to them?'

'What happens to anybody? They died.'

Christmas with the Dragon must have been a come-down after all that, but I looked forward to it every year, for I also had some pretty dresses (which used to belong to my sister Doris) which I liked to put on and her crockery was so lovely it was a pity to put food on it, and there was always the Christmas tree with the fairy lights, and the open fire, and the roast turkey and the mince pies and the Christmas pudding and the fruit and the drink, and amid all the colour and warmth, even the Dragon sometimes began to look human, or maybe it was the drink (that is the drink she had) for she could smile and be pleasant and even tell jokes.

Then one Christmas eve, as I was helping the Old Woman into her velvet dress, the 'phone rang. It was Emily. She sounded upset.

'Could you come over, Phyllis, quick. Mrs Kilpatrick's turned funny.'

I rushed over as fast as I could and found her stretched out on the couch in a long silk dress, her eyes shut, her mouth and chin quivering. Emily stood there wringing her hands, but keeping her distance, as if the Dragon might explode. I don't know why she had 'phoned me, she should have 'phoned an ambulance. So I called one and then a doctor. They arrived together about half an hour later and took her away.

The Dragon survived, but without the fire, and came back a grey heap, and Emily almost had to lift her in and out of her chair, and although she was no longer shouted at or bullied, she became more of a slave to her than ever. She became thinner, her hair turned grey, and she seemed to have less and less time for me. She even stopped going to church because she couldn't leave the Dragon on her own. I offered to look after her, but she said: 'No, Phyllis, you wouldn't know how to handle her.'

'I can't see that it'll make any difference to her, she doesn't know one face from another.'

'Oh, but she does. She wouldn't let anyone touch her. The vicar's wife tried to feed her the other day. She began shaking and shuddering as if she was going to have a fit.'

'I'd also shake and shudder if that woman tried to feed me,' I said, but she still wouldn't let me go near her.

She moved from her small room into the Dragon's bedroom and didn't have any rest day or night and hardly stepped out of the house.

'This can't go on,' I told her, 'you'll go to pieces.'

And she did. She had a cold which she neglected and a few days later she caught pneumonia. I suppose she might have died from it if I hadn't called a doctor. She was taken to hospital, and so was the Dragon. When she came out three weeks later looking weak, pale and shaken, the Dragon was dead, but she hadn't been told anything about it, and when she came back to the Crescent, she found the house in darkness, the blinds drawn, and the doors locked and bolted. She had no money, nowhere to go, nothing to do, and she couldn't even get out the few belongings she had in the house, and the Old Woman played the good Samaritan and took her in for a bit.

After a day or so she began to regret her good deed and so, to be honest, did I.

We had three comfortable, empty rooms upstairs, but she was put in the fourth, the attic, which was more of a box-room than anything else, but which did happen to have a bed, and she was overcome with the Old Woman's kindness.

'Oh, it's ever such a nice room, so spacious, so lovely, and the view.' At first the Old Woman thought she was being ironic, but she gushed like that about almost everything. She couldn't get over the fact that the Old Woman sat with us in the kitchen, and was half afraid to touch her food until the Old Woman lost patience and told her to get on with it.

We have two television sets, a large coloured one which was in the Old Woman's room, and a small black and white one, in the living room. The Old Woman had an annoying habit of giving a running commentary on everything she saw, so that as a rule I was normally content to watch the black and white, even though it always looked as if it was snowing and the picture had a habit of jumping up and down, but if there was anything I particularly wanted to see I would knock on her

31

door and, if she was in a good mood – which she sometimes was, especially after a meal – she'd let me come in and watch.

Well, that particular night, there was something I particularly wanted to see, so I asked Emily to come with me to the Old Woman's room.

'Oh, I can't.'

'Why not?'

'It's her private room, her bedroom.'

'So? We'll only be watching her television, we won't be getting into bed with her.'

'But it's taking a liberty.'

I finally almost had to twist her arm to get her up the stairs. Well, we were settled and watching an old film (my favourite television) with Barbara Stanwyck (my favourite film star) and enjoying it, when I heard someone sobbing in the darkness, and I turned round to see Emily with tears pouring down her face, and before I could say anything she rushed out of the room and upstairs to the attic.

'The girl's hysterical,' said the Old Woman, 'I don't want her in here again.'

I rose and went after her. She was lying face downwards on the bed, drenching the counterpane with her tears.

'It's a sad film,' I said, 'but not that sad.'

She sat up, her face swollen and blotchy.

'I wasn't crying about the film. I was thinking about poor Mrs Kilpatrick, dying like that on her own.'

'Mrs Kilpatrick? She's been dead for three weeks.'

'I know, but I can't help thinking about it.'

'Look, she wouldn't have wasted many tears on you.'

'Yes, but think of the poor woman.'

'I don't want to think of the poor woman, she was an awful old hag, like a walking piece of night.'

'How can you talk like that about the dead?'

'Well, it's true. She treated you like a skivvy when you were alive, and it looks as if she's holding on to you even from the grave. It annoys me the way you go on.'

But the more I went on, the more she sobbed. I was afraid if

I stayed there I would hit her with something, and went back downstairs.

She woke me the next morning with a cup of tea. At first I thought I was dreaming because I'm not used to people bringing me tea in bed, but when I realized that I was awake I nearly threw the tea in her face.

'What's this in aid of?'

'I'm sorry for making myself a nuisance.'

'What nuisance?'

'Last night. I must have spoilt your evening.'

'I wish you'd stop apologizing all the time.'

'Do I apologize all the time?'

'You do nothing else.'

'I'm sorry.'

That afternoon, while the old Woman was asleep, I told her to make some effort to get the Dragon out of her mind. 'She could mess up your whole life if you go on like this. Her death is the best thing that could have happened to you. You're a free woman now, don't you realize it? You can start a new life.'

'Doing what? I'm over sixty, you know.'

It was a fair point, especially as at the moment she looked over seventy.

She busied herself cleaning and scrubbing, usually things I had only just cleaned and scrubbed myself, and though it was a large house she somehow managed to get in the way and had an awkward habit of stepping on Rigby and Digby. She would also jump to her feet every time the Old Woman came into a room, as if she was in the presence of royalty, which startled the Old Woman and so got on her nerves that she kept whispering to me from the side of her mouth:

'I want that stupid cow out of here.'

It was awkward. The poor girl spent half the day scanning the papers and writing off for jobs, or 'phoning for them, but nobody so far even called her for an interview, which didn't surprise me. It didn't surprise her either, but at this rate she could be with us for good.

After she had been with us about a month, the Old Woman said:

'I can't take it any more, neither can Rigby or Digby. The church has all sorts of sanctuaries for waifs and strays. I want you to talk to the vicar. This isn't a rest home for elderly unemployables.'

'She makes herself useful, you know. She hardly rests at all.'

'It wouldn't be so bad if she did, but it's her restlessness which gets on my nerves. She'll have to go, and by the end of this week at the latest. If I wake up next Sunday and she's still here I'll have to throw her out, and you with her.'

And then, as if in answer to a prayer, Emily had good news. She had two older sisters, both of them church missionaries, and both of them working abroad. One of them had just retired and had bought a cottage in Lincolnshire.

'She's asked me to come and stay with her, and one never knows, I may have more luck in Lincolnshire and find something useful to do.'

'Do you mean you're leaving us?' asked the Old Woman, her voice so full of regret you could have thought she meant it.

'I'm afraid I must, I haven't seen her in years.'

But even so another week passed before she finally left.

I missed Emily more than I thought I would and the Old Woman, for her part, missed the Dragon. In a way, I suppose, I did as well. The Tuesday and Thursday tea-parties were not only pleasant but helped to break up the week. The Old Woman still asked me to make cucumber sandwiches and she still ordered walnut cake, but it was not the same eating them in your own house. The week suddenly became terribly long.

It was also nice to know that there was another private house in the street inhabited by another private individual. The Dragon was hardly dead before we heard that her house was to be converted into an hotel, and a month or two later it was under scaffolding and being pulled inside out. The Old Woman and I sometimes stopped on our morning's walk to see the men at work and watch the last remnant of the Dragon's world being torn apart.

'We'll be the last private house in the Crescent,' said the Old Woman, half proudly, half with regret.

One house had been converted into a drawing

office; another into a solicitor's office; a third was the local branch of a trade union; a fourth, which looked as if it was ready to fall apart, was a dame's school; a fifth, with grubby venetian blinds in every window, seemed to have no life in it at all; a sixth was an insurance office; so was the seventh; the eighth was used by some sort of mysterious religious sect. There was hardly any life in any of them after dark, or at weekends, and not all that much life in them during daylight. It was almost as if I was seeing them for the first time now. Until the Dragon died it hadn't really occurred to me how dull and depressing they were.

'We'll keep the flag flying for a bit yet,' said the Old Woman.

Emily wrote to me about once a month to say that she was comfortable (I couldn't imagine her saying anything else) and that she had plenty of time for reading, but that she was having some trouble with her eyes. She had, much to her surprise, been left some money by the Dragon – fifty pounds and a stuffed pike. Most of the Dragon's money – and, according to the Old Woman, it was 'a very, *very* large sum' – had been left to a nephew who, as far as we knew, had never set foot in her house.

When December came and we were due to make our trip to London for the Christmas shopping, the Old Woman was in two minds about going. 'Everything's so expensive, and I suppose I'll have to pay the whole cost of the journey instead of half, unless Ritchie can be persuaded to charge less. There are only two of us travelling instead of four.'

'But he didn't charge more because there were four of you travelling instead of two.'

I'm not sure what arrangement she finally came to but Ritchie drove us as usual, but shopping was not quite the same. The Old Woman complained about the prices as she did every year ('But this is ridiculous . . . robbery . . . you can't be serious . . . Is this pounds or shillings?') and I suppppose she enjoyed the excitement and bustle, but in the past she and the Dragon would always bump into someone they knew. This time there was no one, as if she was carrying out an important religious duty with no one to bear witness. She bought me my usual bottle of Guinness (hidden under fancy wrapping paper) but I can't see that she had to travel specially to London for that.

'It strikes me that English people don't do their shopping in London any more,' she said as we drove home. 'The place is full of foreigners. Only natural I suppose. They're the only ones with the money.'

In previous years she and the Dragon would spend the journey back discussing their plans for Christmas. Now she kept off the subject. I was afraid we might be spending Christmas on our own and so, I suppose, was she. Coggeshall had been down on a visit the previous week and the Old Woman had told him all about 'poor Mrs Kilpatrick. She was so kind, so hospitable. Christmas wouldn't have been Christmas without her,' which was as clear a hint as any that she would have welcomed an invitation, but it passed over him. And then, when I was about to give up hope, we got an invitation from the vicar.

At first I thought she might refuse. She wasn't much of a church-goer, slept through the sermons when she did go, and always complained about them and about the vicar, but when the invitation came she thought we should accept. 'I don't want to offend the man, not at this time of the year.'

There was a laden Christmas tree, and streamers, and the tables were nicely laid out, but there was the decaying smell you always get whenever any number of old people come together, and the place was full of them, old men leaning on walking sticks, old women lolling in wheel chairs, some with deaf-aids, all of them in paper hats and talking at the tops of their voices.

We took one look and were about to do an about turn when the vicar, who had seen us the moment we arrived, greeted us with a loud: 'Ah, there you are, so glad you could come,' grabbed hold of the Old Woman's chair and wheeled her to the top table. The evening had not quite begun, but some of the guests were already helping themselves to anything within reach on the tables.

36

As I sat down I noticed that there were some younger people around, mostly helpers, eager-faced with loud voices and very friendly, in fact too friendly:

'And what do they call you my dear? Phyllis? Now, isn't that a lovely name. I'm Samantha. I'd much rather be called Phyllis. And tell me, what would you like in your Christmas stocking? A bottle of gin? I'm not sure if Father Christmas goes in for that sort of thing, but we'll keep our fingers crossed, shall we?'

The Old Woman was separated from me and was sending out distress signals from her place by the vicar, but there was nothing I could do. Besides, I was in trouble myself.

I found myself hemmed in between two large black women in loud dresses. Blacks are supposed to be easy-going and good company, but I found the going heavy. They looked at me, and I looked at them, and after scratching around for something to say, I turned to one and said: 'What is Christmas like in Africa?' She turned to her friend as if she hadn't heard me.

'She wants to know what Christmas is like in Africa,' said her friend.

'How should I know what Christmas is like in Africa?'

'I don't know how you should know, I'm only saying she wants to know.'

'Lady, I don't know what Christmas is like in Africa.'

There was plenty of food about but the only drink was lemonade and the Old Woman didn't touch a thing, and we fled as soon as we could, though not before the vicar had put on a Father Christmas outfit and given all of us our gifts. I got a life of St. Francis, and the Old Woman a book called '*Third World Christians*', with a picture of a black Jesus on the cover. As we were leaving the vicar's wife was organizing a game of blind-man's buff.

'A workhouse treat,' said the Old Woman disgustedly. 'I don't know what made you want to go.'

'Made *me* want to go?'

'I went for your sake. I have nothing to do with the vicar. He's your friend.'

We were going down a steep hill towards home at the time

37

and I stopped for a bit, wondering if I should let the wheelchair go and let her hurtle all the way down, into the river.

She only had seventeen Christmas cards that year and six of them were from traders. Of the others one was from her solicitor, Coggeshall, who was as good as a trader, one was from me, another from Emily, and the rest were from what I called the Crossley club.

Crossleys had a winter sale every January, but the day before the sales they had a sort of preview for account customers which was like an annual reunion of the local gentry. Many of them were old, or very old, some were in wheelchairs or hobbled around on sticks, most looked as if they had seen better days and they spent more time in the tea-room than the sales floor. They didn't buy that much because Crossleys, at sales times, was more expensive than most other shops all the year round. Emily used to love it because, as she said, even the sales staff seemed to have been well brought up, 'and they made you feel a lady.'

The Old Woman used to prepare herself for the preview as if it was a wedding, or a visit from Coggeshall, and she would spend hours choosing the right outfit, which is not surprising because she had outfits going back sixty years. She also expected me to put on my fancy best, which wasn't always fancy enough for her, and she would ask what I did with all the clothes she gave me, meaning her cast-offs. But by the time she cast off anything it was ready to fall apart, and even if it wasn't you could have got three of me into any of her dresses and so I would pass them on to jumble sales and church bazaars. In any case I still had all the fancy frocks left to me by my poor sister Doris.

We would get most of our groceries from a supermarket, but the Old Woman would telephone a small weekly order to the food department at Crossleys and would sit by the front window waiting for their purple and gold van, with the royal crests on the side, to pull up.

I suppose for the Old Woman, the Crossley preview was, after Christmas, the most important day of the year and when the Dragon was alive they would live off it for a month before and a month or two after, talking about who they had seen, how they looked, what had been happening to them,what was likely to happen, and who they hadn't seen and why they hadn't, and they spoke in what they thought were lowered voices so that Emily and I shouldn't hear:

'Didn't you know, dear, they've gone bankrupt.'

'Oh, so it's true.'

'I wouldn't swear to it, but that's what everybody's been saying.'

'There's no smoke without fire.'

'Exactly.'

But more usually they were simply dead and I suppose the preview was a sort of roll-call of survivors.

With the Dragon dead, preview day was not what it was.

The two would always leave their wheelchairs, and would support each other arm in arm, stomping their sticks in unison, like girls of the old brigade, though they sometimes looked as if they were taking part in a three-legged race.

The Old Woman on her own wasn't quite the same. The Dragon had eyes like a hawk and acted as their look-out. She'd give a cry at the sight of anyone familiar and they would make straight for him. The Old Woman herself was short-sighted, but didn't like to wear glasses, at least in public, and so she stood around by herself, leaning on her sticks, screwing up her eyes and turning this way and that to see if there was anyone she knew. From time to time someone came up to her, which more or less made her day, but she was looking for someone to chat with in the tearoom and was not too pleased when she was left with me.

As she had hardly seen anyone she kept going on about the people she hadn't seen, the Hon. this and Lady that, or Mrs something-or-other, and would not have been interested even if I had, all I could do was grunt, though to vary it I would come up with an 'Is that so?', or 'Well, I never,' which did not satisfy her either, and after a bit she said:

'Talking to you is like talking to a wall. I'd be better off talking to the dogs,' and talk to them she did as soon as she got home, and to be honest, Rigby and Digby seemed more interested in her chatter than I was.

After that Christmas dinner the Old Woman was cross not only with the vicar but with Christianity, and vowed never to set foot in his church again. Not that she had been a regular in the best of times, 'there's no one worth talking to in church any more,' she would complain. While in the past she hadn't gone because she couldn't be bothered, now she stayed away on principle, so when I put on my fancy best to attend Holy Communion on Good Friday she thought I was being disloyal to her. But I liked going to church. It was about the only way I had of knowing that Easter had come, and I liked Easter because once it had come I felt we were over the hump. The worst months of the year were from January to April.

The Old Woman liked to get out for an airing at least once a day, usually right after breakfast, when she would take Rigby and Digby on her lap and I would push her uphill to the park, and in the summer we would sometimes get out in the evening as well, but if it rained, snowed or was icy, we would be stuck inside and she and the dogs would snarl and snap all day. Sometimes we were snowed in for whole weeks at a time, and if it wasn't for Crossleys' van we would have had no way of telling that there was still life in the outside world, which, I suppose, was one of the reasons why she still kept an account with them.

It wasn't so bad when the Dragon was alive, for they could always chat on the 'phone and her house was so near that they could keep up their visits even in bad weather, but with the Dragon dead, and the weather deadly, every week seemed to have thirty days and she became impossible. And after a bad winter her foul temper could last well into the spring.

One morning I brought her her usual cup of tea, and opened the curtains. She turned her head and looked at me with one eye.

'Why did you wake me so early?'

'It isn't early.'

'It's still dark.'

'It's raining, that's why.'

'I don't suppose we'll be able to get out.'

'Probably not.'

40

'Then what was the point of waking me?'

'You don't want to stay in bed all day, do you?'

At which she sat up.

'That's not for you to say. If I want to stay in bed all day, I'll stay in bed all day, you're not my nanny. Veronica was absolutely right. She kept telling me that I had spoilt you, and I obviously have. If I'd treated you like she treated Emily you'd have known your place. Now close those curtains and take that tea out of here before I throw it at you.'

And that was about nothing. When she had something to complain about she could go on about it all day and half the night, and sometimes did. A woman has to have something to do with herself and I suppose it was her way of passing the time.

We usually got our meat in Lamb's. It was a nice shop, with brightly coloured tiles, conveniently situated on the way to the park. It was never particularly busy and we used to drop in for a bit of beef or mutton, and old Mr Lamb, in an apron and boater, would come in from the back shop to serve her in person. When the weather was bad, I had to go on my own and, no matter what the order, she would always warn me: 'Don't over-spend, it's my money, not yours.'

She was never pleased with whatever I got. 'Is that all they gave you? When I first married you could buy a fully grown ox for half the money and still have change for the trimmings,' as if I was in league with old Lamb to rob her. I was in fact very careful with what I bought. Once there was a strike or something, and the price of the usual cuts almost doubled overnight, so I got one of the cheaper sort. She looked at it as if it was something the cat brought in.

'Do you expect me to eat this?'

'It's meat.'

'It's offal' (or maybe she said 'awful').

'It's the best he could do for the price.'

'Well it isn't good enough, you should have told him that. Take it right back.'

'Take it back yourself.'

'If I could have gone out myself I wouldn't have sent you

in the first place. You can no longer be trusted with the simplest errand. I have to get everything, do everything myself, which wouldn't be so bad if you weren't so sullen and peevish and insolent. You're impossible to talk to, impossible to be with and useless. I don't know why I keep you. Charity, I suppose. Veronica always said . . .' And, as usual, after she starts snarling, Rigby and Digby join in with their snarls so, by the time she had finished, I was ready to stifle her with her own dogs.

She'd never, of course, apologize or admit to being in the wrong (neither would I but then I never was in the wrong), but sometimes, when she thought she'd overdone it, she would sidle up to me and say, 'there's a good programme on television tonight, you can watch it in my room if you want.' If I took up the invitation, she would take out a box from a small cupboard near her bed, and offer me a mouldy chocolate.

She must have thought that chocolates were like wine and improved with age. Some of them, I could swear, were pre-war.

4

THE FIRST SUNDAY in June and we were off to Frinton for a month. It was usually chilly and sometimes wet in June, but in July the hotel rates went up and stayed up until September, and so it was always June and always to the same hotel, the Queen Anne, owned by an old soldier, which was full of old soldiers or, more usually, their widows, and old dogs. I don't know if children weren't allowed in the hotel, but I can't remember seeing any, which was perhaps just as well, for the place was like an armoury with daggers and crossed swords on the walls, and shields and muskets and banners and flags. The dining rooms were lined with photographs of regimental groups, and the bedrooms were not numbered but were all named after famous battles. We always stayed in the same room, the Inkerman. It was one of the smaller and less expensive rooms and looked out over the back lawn, so that it must have been a small battle. The larger rooms, which looked out towards the sea, were all named after major battles like Trafalgar and Waterloo. There was a well-stocked library full of regimental histories, and the bar was called the Mess and they used shell-casings as ash-trays. The walls were panelled, and the floors were carpeted. The voices were noisy, but not used much, and even the dogs were quiet and there were times when you could hear a pin drop, as if the two minutes' silence for armistice day had been stretched to the whole year. The first time I came I thought it was the sort of place old warriors went to when they died. Since then they have brought in a few novelties like the television room, which don't really go with the place.

If Christmas and the Crossley preview were the highlights of the winter, Frinton was the highlight of the summer and the Old Woman got really excited once the packing started, like a child getting out her buckets and spades. She began making lists of the things she would need the first Tuesday after Easter Monday, her summer frocks and her summer hats and her summer shoes, though about the only thing she really needed was her fur coat.

It was a peculiar sort of fur, long-haired and greyish brown in colour, and she wore it most days of the year, sometimes even in the house when she thought it wasn't cold enough to have the heating on, but too cold to have her coat off. She said it was lion-skin, but the sort of lions you saw in the zoo didn't have the sort of fur she had on her back, and I thought that it was maybe made up of cats or rabbits, but again the hair was too long, and the colours didn't fit. I sometimes saw that sort of fur on other old bags of about her age – but on nobody younger or better-off – and it seemed to me that the animal had been specially bred for the elderly daughters of well to do families who were no longer doing so well.

Ritchie would take us all the way, which was expensive, especially as his car sometimes broke down and all three of us would have to stay in an hotel overnight. Then we continued by train, she travelling first class and me second, but when she needed me she couldn't get to me, so once, and once only, we both travelled second class, but she found the carriage too crowded, and the people too noisy and too smelly (I asked her if she'd ever taken a whiff at her fur, or, for that matter, at Rigby and Digby). After that it was Ritchie all the way.

The same people used to come about the same time year after year, so that it was like an old boys', or rather, old girls' reunion and, as they only saw each other I don't suppose they noticed how the years were creeping up on them. Several were in wheel chairs and came with their own attendants, or pushers, as we called each other, but the pushers didn't last as long as the pushed, so that you did see a new face every now and again.

Among the regulars was a very old, ashen-faced man with a black beret and a white beard, known as the Admiral. He

44

could not have been an easy man to get on with because he had a new pusher every year, and he couldn't have been an easy man to look after, for he not only had to be pushed, but he had to be fed. His pushers were usually old sailors, breezy, red-faced men – 'A bit noisy and a bit coarse,' the Old Woman would complain – but they were full of jokes and they livened the place up a bit.

One year he came with somebody completely different, a tall, stooping man, with short grey hair standing on end, in a dark, crumpled suit. He kept looking in my direction at meal times, even when he was feeding the Admiral, so that more food went on to the Admiral than into him.

One evening I popped out to a beach shelter for a quick smoke and was just lighting my cigarette when I saw the Admiral's pusher ambling towards me. He was wearing an old army great-coat with his collar turned up, but the first thing I noticed about him were his boots. They were huge, with one turned in one direction and one in the other, while he moved along somewhere between them. He stopped when he saw me, hesitated for a moment, and asked if he could sit down.

'There's nothing to stop you,' I said. And he sat down, with his hands on his knees, staring straight ahead of him, as if he was looking for a ship far out on the horizon. A mist was spreading in from the sea.

'Have you been with the Admiral long?' I asked.

And he turned to me as if he'd seen me for the first time.

'My wife was his housekeeper. I was his handyman myself. He was at Jutland, the Admiral.' He had a bit of a stutter and kept stumbling over his 'm's and 'p's.

'At Jutland?'

'The battle of Jutland. A bit before my time. He used to talk about it all the time, but he's given up talking more or less. He's given up almost everything if it comes to that.'

'Is your wife still his housekeeper?'

'No, no, no, she's not. He hasn't got a house you see, not the big house he used to have; he lives with his sister, and she's getting on.'

'Your wife or his sister?'

'No, no, the sister. The wife's dead.'

'Whose wife, yours or the Admiral's?'

'No, he never had a wife, the Admiral. It's my wife what's dead. He'll be a hundred next year, the Admiral.'

'Is he difficult?'

'Difficult?'

'The Admiral.'

'No. Dead easy. Sleeps most of the time. If I didn't wake him for meals he'd probably sleep for good.'

His name was Walter and he had been with the Admiral since the war.

'There was seventeen of us working for him at one time, five in the house and twelve in the grounds. They're all gone now. The house is gone, the grounds is gone, there's only me and him and his sister living in the lodge and a woman who comes in to cook and clean. Horrible woman, horrible cook. Pinches half the food. She thinks I don't know what's happening, but I'm not as thick as I look.'

'And all you do is look after the old man?'

'No, he's got a bit of a garden and I look after that, and there's medals to polish. Hundreds of them. Come Remembrance Sunday and it takes me half the morning to put them on. And then there's his stars and crosses and sashes and belts, and his sword. That takes a bit of polishing, his sword, and it's a nuisance cause it gets caught up in the wheels.'

'Has your wife been dead long?'

'Two years, nearly three. She was a bit silly about mushrooms. Liked to collect her own, but she was getting a bit short-sighted and picked up some poisonous toadstools. Good job she ate them first, otherwise we'd all be gone.'

The next day I was pushing the Old Woman along the front. She was wearing her fur coat, fur hat and fur gloves, with a heavy travel rug about her legs and Rigby and Digby snuffling and snorting on her lap. I hadn't gone far when I heard the rapid clip-clop of heavy boots behind me, and a minute later the Admiral and Walter drew up alongside.

'Would you like to have a race?' said Walter.

'A race? Your Admiral would make you walk the plank if he knew.'

'He's asleep.'

I looked at the Old Woman. She was also asleep, snoring loudly with her mouth open. The dogs too were snoring and asleep.

'All right,' I said, 'to the clock. Get ready, get set, go.'

The pavements were nearly empty and those few people about scattered and shook their sticks angrily at us. The dogs woke and began yapping excitedly. Rigby got so excited that he toppled off, right in the path of the Admiral. Walter tried to avoid him but too late. The chair went right over the dog and toppled over and the Admiral went tumbling out into the path of an oncoming car. The car managed to stop in time but all the noise and commotion woke up the Old Woman.

I was afraid we had killed Rigby, but he seemed none the worse for his mishap, and neither for that matter, was the Admiral, though it was hard to tell, but the Old Woman was furious. Her face turned red, her fur bristled.

'I've known you to be nasty, spiteful and useless, but never irresponsible. You could have killed me, and the dogs. Poor Rigby, poor Digby. I shall advertise for a new companion as soon as I get back home.'

We had been through all that before, so it didn't worry me, but she wouldn't speak to me at supper and later in the evening, when I asked her if she wanted help in the bath, she said: 'No thank you, I feel safer on my own,' and for the first time I began to wonder whether she had really meant it.

That night I was watching television. It was pouring outside so the television room was full, but it emptied as the night wore on and by about ten I was on my own, or I thought I was, until I looked round and noticed Walter sitting behind me. I hadn't seen him come in. A little later – again without my noticing – he had moved beside me, but I forgot he was there for I was concentrating on the film. It was an old film, and I loved old films, in fact they're about the only thing on television that I like. Anyway, there was Merle Oberon being held in Laurence Olivier's arms and his lips were moving to

47

hers when I felt a heavy, moist hand sliding under my skirt. I jumped a bit and looked round. It was Walter, his eyes on the screen, but his hand seemed to have a life of its own, as if it didn't belong to him. Normally I'd have given him one between the eyes, but I honestly wasn't sure if he knew what his hand was doing. And in any case I wasn't sure I wanted him to stop. It was a long time since anyone had done that to me, and that was during the war in an air-raid shelter after the light had blown, and whoever it was who was doing it couldn't have known who he was doing it to (and I was afraid to find out because my brother Arthur was on leave at the time and I rather think it was him). But then, as his left hand was busy under my skirt, his right hand began to fumble in his trousers, which was a bit too much, because apart from anything else the door wasn't locked and anyone could have walked in.

'Keep your hands to yourself, you dirty old bugger,' I said, at which his hands flew back as if they were on springs. And he not only moved his hands back, he moved to a far corner of the room. A few minutes later I heard a sobbing noise coming from the back and looking round I saw him heaving with tears.

Since I had never seen a fully-grown man sobbing before I wasn't sure what to do, but as he kept on heaving and shaking I turned down the television and went over to him.

'I'm sorry,' I said, 'I didn't mean to upset you.'

'I was only being friendly,' he sobbed, 'that's all. I thought you wouldn't mind.'

'But you were taking a bit of a liberty, weren't you?'

'I was only trying to be friendly.'

'You can be friendly with a woman without putting your hands up her skirt you know. Besides, anyone could have walked in. This is a public room.'

'I haven't got a private room. I sleep with the Admiral.'

'He must be about as mean as the Old Woman,' I said. 'That's how the rich stay rich.'

Then a thought occurred to him.

'He's ga ga, you know, the old Admiral. He wouldn't know what was happening even if he saw what was happening, if you see what I mean.'

I saw what he meant and was pleasantly shocked. It was the first time for as long as I could remember that I had received an invitation to do something I shouldn't, but I hardly knew the chap and as I sat there thinking about it, he began sobbing again.

'Nobody lets me near them.'

'Come on,' I said, 'it's not that bad. You only feel like that because you miss your wife!'

'No I don't. She didn't fancy it. Never laid a finger on her.'

'You didn't?'

'Not once.'

'How long were you married?'

'Thirty-five years.'

'Poor man.' And I took his hand and put it under my skirt. 'Is that better?'

'Much better.'

I should have heard the stomping of her sticks, but I didn't, and at that moment the door was thrown open and the Old Woman stood in the doorway.

'Am I interrupting something?' she asked. I would have liked to say as a matter of fact you are, but being brought up the way I was I quickly jumped to my feet and straightened my skirt. The room was dimly lit, so I don't know if she had seen anything, not that there was all that much to see, but it wouldn't have done her any harm to know that even at fifty-five I could still attract men who wanted to put their hands up my skirt.

'It's my back,' she said. 'It's playing me up again.'

She often had trouble with her back, and a woman in a neighbouring town used to come over and massage it for her, but since she thought she was too expensive I had to do it instead. At first I wasn't sure what I was meant to do, neither was she, so I would sit astride her and pummel her back as if I was kneading dough. I did it this time with a vengeance, and she was screaming for me to stop long before I had finished, but it worked, or at least she said it did, or perhaps the original pain in her back now seemed quite minor compared to the new pain I had given her.

'Are you going to bed now?'

'No,' I said, 'I'm going out for a smoke.'

'But you disturb me when you come in late.'

'Then you should have got yourself a separate room, shouldn't you?' And I rushed out still hoping to find Walter. Once the hotel was asleep we could do what we liked, but he had gone to bed.

The next morning at breakfast he came over to me looking rather upset.

'The Admiral's been difficult. He didn't want to get into his bath. He didn't want to get out of his bath. He didn't want to get dressed. He didn't want to get into his chair, and now he's not taking his breakfast.'

I went over to see what I could do, but as I tried to force a spoonful of semolina between his lips, I noticed that his lips were blue, and his eyes were glazed. 'I may be wrong,' I said, 'but I think he's dead.'

Walter said he would write, but the poor man was so upset and confused by the turn of events that he probably lost my address. When a month had passed and I had still heard nothing from him I thought I would write him a note to ask how he was doing. I wasn't sure if I was doing the right thing, and after I had posted it I was sorry I had written it. Anyhow he didn't write back. And come to think of it, I wasn't even sure if he could write, though I sometimes wondered if he had written and the Old Woman had picked up his letter and burnt it. I wouldn't have put it past her. She dived on the post as soon as it came: it was about the only thing which could make her move with any speed. I suppose she was afraid that if I'd got my hand on her letters, I'd steam them open. Not that she got that many. They were mostly bills, or the sort of long envelopes solicitors send, or very large envelopes with annual reports of this or that. Private letters she hardly got at all.

I think she guessed there had been something between Walter and me and, sometimes at supper, if she thought I was off guard, she'd try to see what she could find out.

'It was sad the Admiral dying suddenly like that, wasn't it?'

'He was nearly a hundred, what do you expect?'

50

'But it quite spoilt the holiday for all of us. It's so depressing when people go suddenly like that, specially after he'd been coming all those years – and you and his companion were getting on so well.'

'His companion?'

'You know, what was his name, the tall gentleman.'

'Walter you mean?'

'Was that his name? He was a widower, I gather.'

'You seem to know more about him than I do.'

'I wonder what he's doing with himself now, poor man. He seemed quite beside himself when the Admiral died.'

But no matter how hard she tried, I didn't let out a thing, which wasn't all that difficult because there was hardly a thing to let out.

The summer passed and the Old Woman began talking about going away at Christmas.

'What's the point of talking about it,' I said, 'you always talk and never go.'

'Well there's the expense to consider, but this year I feel entitled to a Christmas holiday because my summer holiday was spoilt.'

'Can't see why the Admiral dying should have spoilt your holiday. You're still alive – after a fashion. I'd rather stop here.'

And then one morning, over breakfast, she wagged an envelope under my nose.

'A letter for you – who from I wonder?'

I grabbed it from her and put it in my pocket.

'Aren't you going to open it?'

'What business is it of yours?'

'I didn't say it was any of my business, but when I get a private letter I can't wait to open it. You are curious.'

'Not half as curious as you are. And in any case, it's probably a bill.'

'A bill? What bills have you got? I pay for everything.'

I was in fact bursting to know who it could be from, but I had no intention of opening it while she was around, so as soon as I had finished my breakfast I rushed to my room and tore it open. It was from a social worker in a London hospital to say that my brother was seriously ill, and she thought that I might want to see him. She didn't say what the illness was or whether he wanted to see me.

I had been very close to my sister Doris, but not that close to Arthur, partly because he was hardly ever around, and as it was more than twenty years since I had last heard of him I hardly gave him a thought. Now, suddenly, there was this letter and I nearly wept with vexation.

'Now, now,' said the Old Woman, 'It's not like you to get upset like that. They've got the most marvellous medicines these days. They can keep you going forever.'

I could hardly tell her that I wasn't upset so much about hearing from Arthur, as about not hearing from Walter. I wasn't much of a sister, but then he hadn't been much of a brother. News from Arthur was always bad news. It meant that he either wanted something or was on the run from somebody. I sometimes, especially round about Christmas, wondered what he was doing or where he could be, but never tried too hard to find out, for I knew if the worst came to the worst he would always find me.

The Old Woman, in a sudden rush of Christian charity, told me to drop everything I was doing and go straight to the hospital.

'But I'm in the middle of my cooking.'

'Do as I tell you.'

'But —'

'Go!' And for good measure she pushed a small box into my hand.

'What are these?'

'My favourite chocolates. He'll love them.'

'They'll bring on a relapse,' I almost said.

I left feeling bewildered, even slightly suspicious. What had made her so considerate suddenly? Or was she merely up to something and wanting me out of the way?

The hospital, a huge grey building with narrow windows and dark corridors smelling of carbolic and urine, seemed to be falling to pieces and there was hardly a white face around the place. Even the doctors were black. Nobody had heard of the woman who sent me the letter and nobody seemed to know where Arthur was, or even if he was there in the first place, but then, as I was rushing from ward to ward, I happened to notice an elderly, grey-faced man, half-sitting, half-lolling in bed, staring dazedly around him. He looked in my direction once or twice without obvious signs of recognition.

'You're not Arthur are you?' I asked.

He didn't seem to be too sure himself, and I didn't think it could be, if only because he didn't have the usual look of low cunning in his eyes, but Arthur it was. He'd been picked up in the street more dead than alive.

Visiting time was nearly over by the time I got there, but there didn't seem to be much point in staying on, because he obviously didn't know who I was, and when I sat down next to him, he pulled up his blankets, as if afraid I might get in beside him.

I asked the doctor what was wrong with him.

'More a question of what's right with him,' he said, 'but is he only fifty-seven?'

'He is, if he's my brother.'

'Hasn't worn too well, has he? He's had a bout of pneumonia, and everything seemed to seize up for a bit, but now that we've got him ticking over he should probably pull through.'

Which he did, though he wasn't the same Arthur, because he became peevish and sorry for himself, which the old Arthur never was, and began complaining about the things I'd brought him, or the things I hadn't like black grapes, for example.

'They've all got black grapes in this ward, and half of 'em aren't nearly as poorly as I am. Three weeks you've been coming here, and not one sodding grape.'

I brought him grapes the next day and he said they looked as if they'd been sat on, which they probably had, but they were the best I could afford.

'You're living with this old bag who's got everything, hasn't she?' he asked.

'She may have, but I haven't.'

'She wouldn't miss a bunch of grapes.'

By which point I'd had enough.

'Look, you thieving bastard,' I said, 'just because you can't keep your grubby paws off other people's things, it doesn't mean to say I've got to do the same. You've never lifted a bloody finger for anybody, and you expect everybody to do everything for you. Useless, that's what you are and that's what you've always been, though father couldn't see it, too lazy to get a job, and too useless to keep it. You broke poor mother's heart. "Whatever'll happen to poor Arthur," she kept saying to herself. "Whatever'll happen to poor Arthur." It's a mercy she passed on before you got going. We never heard from you, not as much as a Christmas card, and never saw anything of you, till you wanted something from us. You were a disgrace to the family from the day you were tall enough to pick a pocket. Father should have . . .'

I broke off as his shoulders began heaving and tears started pouring down his face.

I sat down on the bed and put an arm round him.

'Come on Arthur,' I said, 'that's not like you. You've never been like that.'

'You're right,' he sobbed, 'they should have left me in the gutter where they found me.'

'No, don't go on like that. You can always make a new start.' I took out a handkerchief and wiped his eyes and blew his nose. I'd always felt like his big sister. I was everybody's big sister, even mother's in a way, though I was the youngest in the family. He was so thin and pale, with washed-out, red-rimmed eyes, and pouches round his mouth that the sight of him broke my heart, but the sound of him, the great, heaving sobs, was even worse.

'Now stop it Arthur,' I said, 'stop it,' and with a bit of effort he gradually pulled himself together. I looked hard for the trace of the lively, mischievous, bright-eyed youngster I remembered, or even the familiar look of low cunning. 'He'll be a station-master one day,' father used to say, 'and not on some forgotten branch-line. Paddington, that's where he'll be.' And here he was with his life behind him and nothing to show for it.

He took one of the grapes and munched it disconsolately.

'Leave them,' I said, 'they're half rotten.'

'They're fine,' he insisted.

'They're rotten,' I said.

'They're fine,' he growled, and we had quite a tussle as I pulled them from his grasp. 'I'll get you better ones tomorrow.'

'Don't,' he said, 'They cost a fortune.'

I left him feeling rather worried.

Arthur was a villain, there was no getting away from that, but at least I had always known him for what he was. Now it looked as if I had a new brother to deal with, a better one maybe, but a different one, and I was a bit too old for changes. Better the devil you know, than the saint you don't know. Not that he was a saint, but he had the half-dead look of one. What could he do with himself at his age? What could I do to help him? I had a bob or two saved up. Perhaps we could set up something together. A shop maybe? Or a boarding-house?

It so happened that Stanley was on one of his periodic visits to the Old Woman and while we were having a bite in the kitchen, I asked his advice. I didn't mention Arthur, but I said I had a bit of money saved up, and asked him what would be the best thing to do with it.

'You mean set up in a small business or something like that?'

'Or something like that.'

'Very sensible of you, very sensible. Mrs Crystal will not last forever so it's about time you gave some thought to your future. What I would do is open a launderette. You need a bit of capital to start with, but the manufacturers lend you the rest. The hours are long, and you may need a partner, preferably someone who knows how to look after the machines, but it can be very profitable.'

It struck me that Arthur might be the very man, for he had always been good with machines, especially when it came to starting up other people's cars without them knowing, and he would probably be equally handy with the washing machines.

I was so excited about the idea that I could hardly sleep. The only thing which worried me was how the Old Woman would take it. She had, for some reason, been particularly nice about

Arthur, so nice in fact that I kept wondering if she was still her old self, or what she would expect in return. She had not only given me a whole box of chocolates for him (which I had finally passed on to an old crock in the next bed), but hadn't complained once about the time I'd spent visiting him, so I could hardly turn round and tell her, 'Good-bye old dear, my brother's better, you can go and get stuffed.' I'd have to wait a bit until I broke it to her, giving her a chance to find a replacement. In the meantime I would have to discuss it with Arthur.

The next morning while she was having breakfast her face suddenly changed colour, and she said: 'Oh dear, I do feel odd.'

I asked if I should call the doctor.

'Yes, do, but only Boxer.'

She had two doctors, MacFadyen, whom she called only when she was seriously ill, and Boxer whom she called when she wasn't. MacFadyen was her private doctor, Boxer was on the National Health. Whatever it was, it meant I couldn't see Arthur that day, and the next day she got so bad that we had to call MacFadyen. She was hot at one moment and cold the next, and sweating so much that I had to keep changing her linen.

'Lots of hot drinks and disprins,' said MacFadyen, cheerfully. 'I'll call again in the morning.'

The way she looked I wasn't too sure if there would be anything to call for, and it seemed to me that the problem of how to break the news to her would soon solve itself.

In the meantime my conscience began smarting. I could always read her mind and it occurred to me that perhaps she could read mine, or perhaps old Stanley had let something slip, but anyhow I had the feeling that my plans had suddenly brought on her illness. I may not have loved the old bird, but I didn't want to kill her, not after she had been so nice about Arthur, so I tried to get the whole business of the launderette out of my mind. 'You're not leaving,' I told myself, 'you're staying put,' and, believe it or not, the next morning she was sitting up in bed, if not completely cured, at least well enough to tell me off for calling MacFadyen instead of Boxer.

The following night I was locking up when there was a knock on the door, and there was Arthur in a black coat several sizes too big for him, and a battered suitcase in his hand. He had just discharged himself from hospital.

'But you don't look well enough to be out.'

'I won't get better staying in.'

'You can't stop here you know.'

'Not even for the night?'

I couldn't disturb the Old Woman but I thought she wouldn't mind if I let him stretch out on the sofa downstairs, and even if she would she didn't have to know, but I told him he would have to be out of the house by seven in the morning.

'I'm an early starter,' he said, 'I'll be on the way long before that. Haven't had a bite all day, though.'

I didn't want to start cooking anything elaborate, for she had a nose like a bloodhound and would want to know why I was making myself meals at this time of the night, so I made him a ham sandwich and a cup of tea. He seemed a bit jittery and so, for that matter, was I; every time we heard a floor-board creaking we both jumped.

He wolfed down the sandwich, and I made him another and a third. I was glad to see that he had at least got his appetite back.

'I had lots of time to think while I was in hospital,' he said, his mouth still full, 'and what you said was right. I'm not much use for anything . . .'

'Oh I wouldn't say that . . .'

'But you did say it, and you was right. I'm not much use for anything, not even as a criminal. Well, I've learnt my lesson. You're looking at a new Arthur. You know where I've been? On the other side, that's where I've been. They gave me up for dead in the hospital, and if I'm still alive, it's only for one reason – to be given another chance, and I've taken it. You see my trouble was I never gave a thought to anybody but myself. Well that's going to change too, and last night I was thinking to myself, could you be happy in what you're doing? I mean do you like skivvying about for the old bag?'

I was so taken back by the question, not because it was odd , but because it was odd coming from him, and I wasn't sure what to say. He answered for me.

'Of course you're not. "She's got her head screwed on has our Phyllis," father always used to say. You was always the brains of the family. Doris was the looks, I was the hands, you was the brains. You don't want to spend the rest of your days looking after that old bag.'

'I'm too old to start anything new.'

'No, you're not. You're only too old if you're dead. We could both make a new start.'

'You know what dad always wanted for you.'

'I know, the railways. I could do better than that. They're for blacks, the railways. I was thinking we could go into business together you and me, open a launderette maybe.'

I was drinking a cup of tea as he was speaking and it fell with a crash to the floor. He jumped a foot in the air and nearly bit his tongue off.

'A launderette did you say?'

'What's wrong with a launderette?'

'It's uncanny, I've been playing with the same idea myself.'

I no longer had a conscience about the Old Woman. If fate wanted me to open a launderette, I'd jolly well open it.

'We'd need a few bob, of course, but I think I know where to find it.'

'I've got a few bob,' I said.

'Yes, but you don't want to touch that.'

'Why not?'

'You're saving it for a rainy day.'

'Is this bright sunshine then? I could draw it out.'

'You mean you don't have it in cash?'

'Never, who does? It's in the Post Office, but once we find a place it wouldn't take me more than three or four days to get it out.'

'It's not worth bothering. I mean how much could you have?'

'Over a thousand?'

'How much?'

58

'Eleven hundred pounds nearly, and she still owes me three weeks wages.'

He too another bite on his sandwich and chewed it thoughtfully.

'No, don't touch it.'

'That's up to me, isn't it? I'll go to the Post Office first thing tomorrow to tell them I want to draw it out, so I could have it all ready in case anything likely turns up.'

'Let's talk about it in the morning,' he said.

I kissed him goodnight, which was something I don't think I'd ever done in my life, and went upstairs to bed. My step felt curiously light, as if I was a new woman. I put my head round the Old Woman's door to see if she was still breathing. She was snoring so loudly the curtains flapped.

I rose early the next morning to make him a cup of tea, but he was already gone. So was about everything of value in the house, including all the silver cutlery, some of the the crockery, salvers, trays, paperweights, candle-sticks, silver, ice-bucket (which we had never used) half a decanter of brandy, an ivory back-scratcher, several ivory fans, an ebony spear, a ceremonial sword and all her dad's medals. He couldn't have carried it all in his case and must have had a van, and maybe an accomplice, waiting outside.

I immediately called MacFadyen.

'Has she had a relapse?' he asked anxiously.

'No, but she's about to have one, and if it comes to that, I'm not feeling too good myself,' and I told him what happened. I then called the police.

They all arrived together about the same time and while MacFadyen was upstairs tending to the Old Woman, the police were downstairs trying to pull me apart. I said I had locked and bolted all the doors and windows, which was perfectly true, but there was no sign of forcible entry, and they grilled me as if I was an accomplice, which in a way I was. I gave them a full description of Arthur, though I didn't tell them he had been in the house.

The Old Woman was in the meantime carted off to hospital and put in an incubator or ventilator or something like that (maybe it was only the elevator, because the hospital was very crowded), and I was left all alone in the huge house.

Towards evening the bell went and I picked up the meat axe, just in case it was my brother coming back for more, but it was two lean little chaps with long noses, and long teeth, like over-grown ferrets, and without a word they walked right past me into the house.

'Where is he?' said the first ferret.

'What are you talking about?'

'Come off it,' said the second.

'You don't mean my brother Arthur, do you?'

'Your brother, is he?' said the first.

'We want to cut his throat,' said the second.

'Not while I'm around, you won't,' I said. 'I'll do it first.'

He had worked in their betting-shop and fled with the takings, but by the time they traced him he was in hospital and not expected to pull through, and when they went to make sure he didn't, he had fled yet again.

They didn't quite take my word that he wasn't around, but having searched the house from top to bottom eventually left, muttering unpleasantly.

'We'll get him yet,' said the first. 'Don't let him think he'll get away with it.'

A little later a taxi pulled up and a larger, straighter version of the Old Woman appeared, but in the same sort of fur coat. It was her sister Mildred. I got a shock because from what I knew she and the Old Woman were hardly on speaking terms. Had she come to take over because the Old Woman had passed on? But it wasn't as bad as that, or not yet.

'Dr MacFadyen called me,' she explained, 'and I felt I should be around till she's better. Would you care to make me a cup of tea, Earl Grey please.'

5

WHAT HAD NEVER occurred to me – and it had certainly never occurred to the Old Woman – was that she would come to stay. The Old Woman valued her privacy and liked to have space, and often said to me: 'I don't like using the spare room because once it's in use I don't have any room to spare,' which would have been reasonable enough if she hadn't had rooms to spare. But I think the robbery had reduced her to a state of shock which left her defenceless against her older sister, and once she had moved in she was in.

Everything changed. I never liked change at the best of times and as far as I was concerned all change was for the worse, but I had never imagined that it could be quite as bad as it actually became.

First there was the change in the very appearance of the place. The walls had been covered with family photographs, old faces mostly, and not particularly pretty ones, but they had become familiar and I had begun to look at them as friends. Now they were crowded out, and in some cases replaced by Mildred's paintings, her own paintings, by which I mean not paintings she owned, but paintings she had painted. She was an artist, or thought she was, and she had covered dozens of canvases, mostly in a dark, sickly green, the colour of steamed spinach. She also replanned the garden, uprooted the red-currant plants on which I had laboured (and which, I will admit, were yet to grow their first currants) and replaced them with bulbs. But worse was to come.

One evening, about a week after the Old Woman had come out of hospital, I noticed that the dining room table was set for two, and the kitchen table for one. Nobody said a word to me about the new order and I had half a mind to sit down at the dining room table and let Mildred or Martha eat in the kitchen, but Mildred took me aside and explained that since she had one or two family matters to discuss with her sister, would I mind eating in the kitchen 'for the time being?' I didn't really mind at first because they had the habit of talking about people I had never heard of, and in whom I wasn't interested, and the meals used to drag on. Now that I was on my own in the kitchen I could get through my supper in a few minutes, but after a week or two I noticed that I was beginning to talk to myself, mainly, I suppose, because I had no one else to talk to, or quarrel with.

In the old days, when I was a maid, the Old Woman used to ring a little bell when she needed anything, and I waited to see if they would do the same now, so that I could let them ring until they and the bell burst, but they knew better. Mildred had got herself a hot plate and everything was ready by the table before they sat down to eat, so they managed without me, though they left me to clear and wash up. There wasn't really all that much to keep me busy any more, because if the Old Woman wanted to go out for an airing, Mildred went with her, and did the pushing, though if it was an uphill push she sometimes asked me to take over.

It took me a long time to get the measure of Mildred. I found it difficult to be rude to her, or answer back, because she was always polite to me and, unlike her sister, she would never poke her nose into my business. In fact, she was something of a lady, which her sister wasn't. I kept wondering what was it that had made them fall out in the first place. Like most English ladies, she had a loud voice and, although I ate in the kitchen, it was not too difficult to follow what was going on in the dining room, and from what I could hear it had something to do with a will. Funerals brought families together, wills tore them apart.

When the first Monday in December came, Mildred and Martha went off to London to do their Christmas shopping without me. Mildred had tried to persuade her sister to leave Digby and Rigby at home, but she said she couldn't. A good job she didn't for I might have done them in.

I was upset at being left out. It wasn't that I was all that keen on London and the crowded shops, but I liked the ride in the car, and I hated to be left behind, and when they came back I wouldn't speak to them, but I don't think they noticed. I didn't have all that much to say at the best of times, and they were so busy talking about things in London that I couldn't have got a word in edgeways even if I had wanted.

It was Christmas in another three weeks. I took it that we wouldn't be going to the vicar again, and they still hadn't said what their plans were. The Old Woman kept talking about going away, though she hadn't said where, and I couldn't see her spending the money, especially as it would have meant taking me with, but now that she had her sister back she could manage without me, and I could see them going off and leaving me, with or without the dogs, on my own.

Emily still wrote to me about once a month and in her last letter she had mentioned that it would be nice if I could come and spend Christmas with her and her sister, Bertha. 'I know it's probably impossible,' she added, 'but it's a nice thought.' I now wrote back to say that I hoped ·to come. After I had posted the letter I wondered if I wasn't being hasty because if the Old Woman could do without me over Christmas, she could probably do without me for good. And in any case I hadn't even mentioned it to the Old Woman. I suppose it was a way of telling myself that if she wasn't dependent on me, I wasn't dependent on her, but when I asked her if I could be away for a few days, she said:

'You don't mean over Christmas?'

'Yes, over Christmas.'

'That's quite impossible. We're having visitors. How do you expect me to manage?'

I perked up at that, especially the idea of visitors. I was curious to see who was coming, but before I could say a word, Mildred chirped in:

'The poor woman's entitled to a few days off at Christmas the same as anyone else. Let her go. We'll manage.'

I didn't like being called 'poor woman' and I was hoping the Old Woman would argue and insist that I had to stay, but I suppose she'd been reckoning up what she would save on food if I was away, and two weeks later I packed a bag and set off for Lincolnshire.

It was an odd feeling. I'd never been away from the Old Woman for more than a day before. I'd never been farther north than Frinton. I set out in the early hours of the morning, while it was still dark, and it was dark again by the time I got to my destination. It hadn't occurred to me that England was that big.

Emily came to meet me at the station.

'Do you believe in prayers?' she said. 'I was praying, praying that you might come, and here you are. Isn't it marvellous? Oh, we shall have fun.' She had put on weight since I'd last seen her, one of her legs was swollen and she was limping.

'Some sort of silly infection, but it's clearing up.'

Her sister, Bertha, lived in an old red brick house on the edge of a small village. She was a sterner version of Emily and also older, taller and larger, with a nose so upturned that when Emily introduced me I found myself looking up a dark pair of hairy nostrils. She wasn't very friendly.

'She's been very busy, writing a book you see,' Emily explained.

'What sort of book?'

'A large one, but I don't know what about, she doesn't like to talk about it.'

From the distance the house looked like a chapel, and it had a churchy smell, as if it hadn't really been lived in, and it was full of mildewed books, but it also reminded me of home because it was so cold.

We weren't poor and we had coal fires and electric heaters, but they were only on in one room at a time and it was only warm in the area round the heater. Elsewhere in the house it was cold and you didn't expect it to be anything else. The Old Woman always complained that the central heating wasn't working properly, but in fact since she had the central heating built I'd forgotten what it was like to be cold, to come into a cold hall, to wake in a cold room, to put your feet down on a cold floor.

And the floor also reminded me of home. There was

linoleum in the passage way, in the bedrooms, the bathroom, and the kitchen, with their patterns rubbed out by repeated scrubbing and polishing.

The downstairs rooms were large and gloomy, and the upstairs rooms were small and gloomy. There were churchy-looking books everywhere, and group photographs of school children, mostly black. Bertha had been headmistress of a mission school in Kenya, and she was in the centre of them all, hair piled high on her head, glasses gleaming, arms folded.

'So you're Emily's friend,' she said. 'She hasn't stopped talking about you, but then she never does stop talking, does she? I sometimes hear her voice downstairs and go down and find the poor girl talking to herself. I'm so glad you could come. It will be nice for her to have company over Christmas.'

She had a study next to her bedroom which she never opened to anybody, and hardly ever came downstairs.

'She's hardly got time,' Emily explained, 'you see she's got this book to write and it keeps her busy.'

She did, however, find time to go to church with us, and in fact church-going was about their main pastime for they had no television. The heating in the church had broken down and the service was taken at a gallop, but the sermon was slow. The Old Woman would have liked the vicar for he was an old man with a tired voice and a lined face, and weary, washed-out blue eyes. Emily introduced me as her best, her very best, friend and it seemed an effort to him to shake my hand.

Emily prepared a fine Christmas meal, with plenty to eat, but only water to drink. Bertha complained about everything, that the soup was too thick, the gravy too thin, the turkey underdone, the pudding overdone. She didn't stir at all during the meal. Emily brought everything and served everybody and took away one course, and brought the next. When it was all over Bertha went to her study while Emily busied herself with the washing up in the kitchen. When I rolled up my sleeves and looked around for an apron, Emily almost screamed: 'You can't do that, you're my guest.'

'Try and stop me,' I said.

It was soon clear to me that Bertha was another Dragon, not

that she shouted or breathed fire, but she expected the same sort of slavery and she got it without even raising her voice. She didn't even have to ask for it, but took it all for granted.

I felt like asking Emily why Bertha, who seemed able-bodied to me, didn't do anything for herself, but I had to mind my own business, and in any case I thought I knew the answer. It seemed to me that Emily could bring out the Dragon in anyone.

In spite of her bad leg she kept jumping up and down, trying to do this or that for me, making cups of tea, clearing the mud off my boots, finding me good books to read, sewing on a button which looked as if it might fall off, so that by the time I left I had got tired of saying 'no' and just let her get on with it.

She had another sister who was also a church missionary and whom she hadn't seen for twenty years.

'I was surprised when she became a missionary,' said Emily, 'for she wasn't really the type. Highly strung and a teeny bit of a bossy-boots, not at all like Bertha.'

I suppose she had been brought up as the family skivvy and after sixty years she couldn't change her ways.

What I liked best about being with her was the chats we had at night after the lights were out. I like chatting in bed in the dark, which was something I hadn't done since poor Doris passed away.

'You and Doris were very close, weren't you?' she said.

'We were and we weren't. You see, Doris was very good looking . . . '

'You're not bad looking yourself, I mean you're not fat like I am, or short-sighted.'

'But she was very good looking. We would often go out together on an evening, but someone would always latch on to her, so that more often than not I came back on my own, but she told me everything.'

'Did she go out with boys on her own?'

'What do you mean on her own?'

'You know, without other people being about, on her own.'

'Yes, but how else do people go out?'

'Was she like the girls in the factory?'

'Which factory?'

66

'The parachute factory I worked in during the war.'

'What about them?'

'Well, you know the sort of things they got up to.'

'You mean . . .'

'Yes.'

'She wasn't an angel, if that's what you mean. As I said, she was very good looking. People looked up when she entered a room – even in church – and she had dozens of boy friends, dozens of them, especially in the war when they built an army camp near us.'

'And did she?'

'Oh yes, many times.'

There was a long, thoughtful silence after that, then she said: 'Have you ever had a boy friend yourself?'

'Well, in a way yes,' and without going into details I told her about Walter, but she wanted details.

'Did . . . did he want to kiss you?'

'No, no, he didn't go in for that sort of thing.'

'No, neither did Horace. He was nice in that way.'

'But he didn't get the chance to try it, did he? You were never alone together.'

'We could have been if he'd really tried, and he didn't. I mean, he was uncouth in some ways, but not in that way, not Horace.'

'You should have married him while the going was good.'

'How could I? What would have happened to old Mrs Kilpatrick if I had?'

'The same as happened to her, though you didn't. I liked Horace, I'm surprised you didn't.'

'Oh, I liked him all right, but as my poor mother used to say, liking is not a good reason for doing something.'

'I can't think of a better one off hand. Weren't you sorry you didn't marry him? Now be honest.'

'Oh but I always am, Phyllis. I was sorry, in a way, especially after poor Mrs Kilpatrick died, and it wasn't all that easy at first here. I can be slow, awkward and forgetful, and though you wouldn't think it looking at her, Bertha can be short tempered, and I kept putting the wrong books in the wrong shelves, and the wrong furnishings in the wrong rooms, but now that we've settled I think it's all for the best. That was another of my mother's favourite sayings, all's for the best.' She hesitated for a moment, and then she said:

'Phyllis, do you think you and I have missed something?'

'What do you mean?'

'Not getting married.'

I thought I knew what she was getting at, but I don't like people beating about the bush, and she was a great bush-beater when it came to some things, so I said to her:

'Do you mean marriage, or the things that go with marriage, because you can have the things that go with marriage without getting married you know. Think what went on in the parachute factory.'

'It wasn't in the factory, it was in the fields at the back.'

'But is that what you're talking about?'

'Yes.'

'Well, to be perfectly honest, I'm not sure if I've missed it altogether.'

She sat up at that.

'Do you mean . . .'

'No, I don't mean – at least not all the way, but I suppose I was about half-way there.'

'What do you mean half-way there? How can you measure these things?'

And I explained what happened in the television room. She was silent for a bit after that, and I thought she wasn't going to speak to me any more, then she said:

'But I thought you said he didn't even kiss you.'

'He didn't.'

'And you mean to say you wouldn't let him kiss you, but you did let him . . .'

'I didn't say I wouldn't let him kiss me. I said he didn't *try* to kiss me.'

'But he did try to . . .

'Yes.'

'And you didn't try and stop him?'

'No, not at first.'

'I didn't think you were like that.'

'I didn't think I was either, but you live and learn.'

I'm an early riser wherever I am, but whatever the time when I came downstairs, Emily was already busy making breakfast. She didn't greet me with her usual bright smile, though, and I wondered if she'd been upset by the things I told her.

'Is anything wrong?' I asked.

'No, it's nothing. Bertha was cross with me, but then she was quite right. I am rather stupid.'

'Why? What did you do?'

'I'd forgotten to lock up last night. Anybody could have walked in just like that, and I daren't think what could have happened. I never usually forget, but it's not often that we have company. I must have got over-excited and forgot.'

'Does Bertha leave everything to you?'

'Small things like that she does.'

'And cleaning, and cooking, and shopping, and washing and ironing.'

'I have the time, and she hasn't.'

'But if you're stupid, or at least, if she thinks you are, why doesn't she lock up herself?'

'How can she? She has so many things on her mind.'

I was waiting for that, in fact I almost said it for her.

After she had cleared up and made the beds and cleaned the rooms (with a bit of unasked for help from me), and after she had made a jug of coffee for her sister (who had not shown her face all morning) we went out for a walk.

It felt odd to be walking like that in the open without pushing a wheel-chair in front of us, but we couldn't go far because Emily's leg was troubling her.

'You wrote that your eyes were giving you trouble,' I said, 'you didn't mention your leg.'

'The leg came on more suddenly. I got up one morning and as I stood up it gave way, but it's clearing up.'

'Couldn't Bertha do some of the household chores until it does clear up?'

'Bertha's an educated woman, Phyllis, she was a headmistress. I'll ask her to show you the photos of some of the

69

girls who have passed through her hands, doctors, dentists and the like. One of them is a radio announcer now.'

I was wasting my breath.

After lunch when Emily rose to clear the table, I got up to give her a hand, but Bertha said:

'I hope you don't mind my saying so, but if you're a guest you should allow yourself to be treated as one.'

'I'm not used to being served hand and foot.'

'Neither is anyone these days' (to which I almost retorted: 'I could name someone who is') and with that she picked up the cup of coffee which Emily had made her, and went to her room.

Why hadn't I answered back? Because I suppose I didn't want to cause trouble for Emily, but I was not used to holding my thoughts back and it was giving me indigestion.

I was telling Emily about Mildred, but she fell asleep in her chair as I was talking, and I was left on my own with my thoughts and my worries. It began to rain and I could hear the muffled sound of the drops falling on the laurel bush outside. Apart from the rain and the ticking and rattling of an old clock on the mantelpiece (it moved, but hardly ever told the right time) there was not a sound to be heard. I couldn't remember it ever being so quiet at Crumpshall because, apart from anything else, the Old Woman and her dogs were noisy even when they slept.

I kept wondering how things were back in 'Eden'. Mildred had said they would manage, but how would they cope with all the cooking and cleaning and clearing up, especially if they had visitors? Mildred may have had the use of her legs, but she was no chicken. Had she piled everything into the sink for me to deal with when I got back? If she had I would tell her what to do with them in words she had never heard before. I had begun to hate Bertha and some of that hatred was so overflowing that I was beginning to hate everybody. There were even times when I felt like taking a frying pan and hitting Emily over her great big stupid head. But the whole place was depressing me, the gloomy, under-heated house and the glum under-heated people, the grey skies and the soggy surroundings. Everything squelched underfoot. The countryside was half covered in mist, which I even felt creeping into my soul. Bertha's years in Africa had done nothing to warm her up, and thinking of her now I almost became fond of the Old Woman, and I even began to think fondly of her dogs. By the end of the day I found myself looking up the notes I had made on the train times back to London.

I had said I was going away for a day or two. 'No, no,' said Mildred, 'you're entitled to a proper holiday, it's Christmas after all. You have a good rest.'

I looked at the Old Woman to see if she would contradict her, but again she didn't say anything, and now that I was away I was beginning to wonder if Mildred had planned what the papers call a 'coup'. She had somehow been able to mesmerize the Old Woman, and I always had the feeling that she wanted to take over the household completely and that she thought that only I stood in her way. Well, if she did, this was her chance, and I suppose if I had been a really dutiful companion – another Emily – I wouldn't have gone away for Christmas, or would have hurried back after a day, but I didn't like the feeling she gave that they could do without me, and so I wanted to stay on as long as possible – at least until all the crockery and cutlery in the house had been used up and was waiting to be washed – if only to teach them a lesson, but after only two days away, it was beginning to hurt me more than it would hurt them. In fact, I was aching to do a bit of washing up.

After supper the three of us sat down to a game of Scrabble. Emily loved the game but she didn't often get a chance to play it. 'Bertha thinks I'm too slow and too stupid and doesn't like to play with me, but I told her you had a marvellous vocabulary.' Emily was slow, but Bertha wasn't that fast, and I'd never heard most of the words she came up with, but after the build up Emily gave me I was afraid to challenge her in case I was wrong, and she led all the way. Towards the end of the game, however, I came up with a seven-letter word which put me slightly ahead and, as the board was tight and she still had seven letters to play, I though I had as good as won, but then, after muttering to herself for about twenty minutes, she came up with 'quammash' which gave her nearly two hundred points, and that much I couldn't take on trust.

'Quammash?'

'Have you never heard of it? It's a sort of lily.'

'Of course I've heard of it, we've got one in our back garden, but is that how you spell it?'

'Are you suggesting I can't spell?'

'No, but perhaps there's more than one way of spelling it.'

'In which case, how would you spell it?'

'Well . . .' I hesitated, for I felt I was taking my life in my hands, 'has it got two "m"s?' Fortunately, it didn't. At which point she shut the dictionary with a bang, rose from her chair and left the room without a word. Emily didn't say anything. She just sat there wringing her hands. Had there been a train available to take me anywhere that night I would have left there and then.

Some time later, as I was getting ready for bed, the 'phone rang. The sound gave me a shock, for though I knew they had a 'phone, it hadn't rung once since I came. I got an even greater shock when Emily said it was for me. It was the Old Woman.

'You'd better come back at once, I'm all on my own.'

'On your own? What about your sister?'

'Never mind my sister. You come right back.'

'Good news?' said Emily. 'You look as if you've had good news.'

I got back on the first train the next day. When I fumbled with my keys in the door the Old Woman came shuffling up to open it and stood in the doorway trying not to look pleased that I was back. Her hands were quivering and, for a dreadful moment, I though she might drop her sticks and embrace me.

6

'DID YOU HAVE a nice Christmas?'

'Yes, very nice. And you?'

'It was lovely.'

'You had guests didn't you?'

'We did on Christmas day, but we went out on Boxing day. I think I may have over indulged myself, because I'm not feeling too good.' She bent down and unlocked her drinks cupboard and brought out my annual bottle of Guinness in a fancy wrapping.

'I haven't forgotten your present,' she said. I opened the Guinness and she gave herself a glass of sherry. I was hoping she might say something about her sister, but not a word, as if she had taken a vow never to mention her name.

A good job I returned when I did because it began snowing that night and continued throughout the next morning and much of the day. I managed to get out to the shops and pick up a few bits of groceries, but by nightfall the streets were piled high with snow and nothing could move.

For a day or two the town, especially the area round the old church, looked like a Christmas card, but then the snow hardened and became grimy. I was nervous of going out and slithered and slipped with every step. As for the Old Woman, she couldn't get out at all, and sat by the windows with the dogs on her lap looking out at the snow, shaking her head, and muttering:

'I won't survive it, not a winter like this,' and I had to remind her that it was still December and that the winter was only beginning. On the morning of New Year's eve she 'phoned Crossleys to order some groceries, and although she waited by the window for much of the morning for a sight of the purple and gold van, it didn't turn up. By lunch-time she was almost in tears and 'phoned to ask what was happening. She was told that all their deliveries were being delayed by the weather. At four they 'phoned to apologize that it would, after all, be impossible for them to make the delivery. I managed to rush out before the shops closed to get the few things we needed, but the Old Woman was distraught. If even Crossleys couldn't get through, the ice-age had come.

And in a way it had. It snowed again during the night and when I tried to get out into the back garden the next morning, to put out some bread for the birds, the door wouldn't open because of the weight of snow piled against it.

I went to the front door and cleared the path, and then cleared away the piled-up snow at the back. It was cold but dry and I began making a snow-man. I had been at it for about twenty minutes when I heard somebody knocking on the window. I looked up and saw the Old Woman gesticulating furiously at me.

'Will you never grow up?' she shouted. I almost thought I heard my mother. When it snowed, Arthur would be out playing all day, but if I joined him I was always told off. 'Have you nothing better to do? Will you never grow up? Stop making a mess of yourself. Come right back inside and make yourself useful.'

The Old Woman went on in the same way, using almost the same words, and I ignored her. When she opened the window to make sure she was heard I threw a snow ball at her. I didn't score a direct hit, unfortunately, but some of the snow did land in her face and she quickly closed the window. About ten minutes later I looked up and there she was in her fur coat, fur hat and fur-lined boots and a snow ball in her hand. She aimed, missed and fell forward on her face. As I bent down to help her up, she pulled me down in the snow and rubbed my face in it, almost burying me. I thought she was angry but then heard whoops of glee and I realized that probably for the first time, and maybe for the last time, in her life she was having

74

fun. I got up and made another snow ball but, before I could throw it, she reached forward with one of her sticks and pulled my legs from under me. I landed with a thump, and she was again upon me pushing snow down my collar, into my mouth, and down my jersey. She wasn't a brigadier's daughter for nothing.

'All right, all right,' I cried, 'I surrender.'

'I'll let you off now,' she said, 'but we'll have a second round tomorrow and it'll be a fight to the death.'

But overnight the temperatures dropped again, quite sharply, and the snow turned to pack ice, and we both stayed indoors.

Crossleys' winter sales were due to begin at the end of the week and the preview was in another two days. If the weather went on like this I wasn't sure if she would be able to get there. The preview brightened her winter and I was afraid to think what she would be like if she had to go through a winter without it, and in fact her first words when she woke and looked out of the window and saw the roads and hedges buried in snow were: 'Oh my God, how will I get to Crossleys?'

But as if by a miracle the weather suddenly changed. The temperature rose, and then the rains came down in a steady torrent. The river overflowed and by the end of the day the town was cut off from the surrounding countryside. But the water went down, the skies brightened and the morning of the preview was like a spring day.

Crossleys was only about half-a-mile away so I could have pushed her there in a wheelchair, but she insisted in arriving in style which meant calling Ritchie. The crowd was not as large as in previous years, and some of the old familiar faces were missing, and several of the old familiar voices were no longer heard, and I thought that the Old Woman came away from the shop looking a little crestfallen. When we got back home she hardly mentioned who she had seen, or any of the gossip she might have picked up. I suppose she still missed the Dragon.

Once the preview was over the Old Woman – who did everything by rote – liked to discuss her holiday plans, and would always begin: 'I think I'll go abroad this year', even though she nearly always ended up in Frinton. When she didn't bring up the subject, I did, but she wasn't interested.

'What's the point of making plans for the summer? Who knows if I'll still be alive then? It mightn't be a bad thing if I wasn't,' and it seemed to me that she was still brooding about the quarrel she had had with her sister.

It was old Ritchie who gave me a hint of what might have happened. He was called out on Boxing day to take them to visit a Mrs Landon. I remembered the name from the Old Woman's Christmas list and she often mentioned her in conversation as a person of some importance.

'They had gone there for tea,' he said, 'and as they wouldn't be stopping for more than two or three hours, and it was a thirty-mile drive, I thought I'd wait for them. Well I suppose I'd been there about two hours when I see the Old Woman dragging herself on her sticks across the gravel, her face as red as a brake light. "Take me home," she says. "Aren't you waiting for your sister?" I says. "Never mind my sister, and do as I say. Take me home." What could I do? I did.'

I could imagine what had probably happened. Doris, my oldest sister, treated me as her best and only friend, as long as no one else was about, but once we had another child playing with us she would have no time for me, or worse, the two of them would gang up against me. It didn't happen often, but it happened often enough to be upsetting. Something like that could have happened here, with her sister and Mrs Landon chumming up together and leaving the Old Woman to shuffle around on her own.

She was a good brooder, the Old Woman, and I thought it would take her a good month to get over it, but she was still moping away in March and if I tried to cheer her up by talking about the summer ahead she only got worse.

Coggeshall came down on one of his quarterly visits, but she didn't even bother to have her hair done and, after the meeting, he took me aside to ask if anything had happened to upset her.

'Something has,' I said, 'but if she hasn't said anything about it to you, she's not likely to say anything to me.'

'Keep an eye her, I think she's sickening for something. Perhaps she could do with a rest.'

'A rest from what?'

'It's been a difficult winter. She can do with a change.'

'The summers aren't all that easy either with her, but you try to speak to her and see what happens. Usually she spends half the winter talking about what she's going to do in the summer, but this year I only have to mention going away, and she bites my head off.'

'She's not as well off as she used to be. Her income's steady, but prices aren't, though I daresay she can still afford Frinton.'

'You talk to her.'

Normally I groaned when somebody mentioned Frinton because we were there nearly every year and I wouldn't have minded seeing some other part of the coast, but I was particularly keen to go this year because I had a feeling that Walter might be there, that in fact he *would* be there. I started working out how, if we didn't go, I might be able to get there just for the day. I had written to Walter but he hadn't answered, and I was sure the reason he hadn't was that he wasn't at his old address and no one had bothered to send on the letter to his new one. He didn't know my address, so he couldn't contact me, but I had told him that we generally went to the same hotel at the same time of the year every year, so that if he did want to contact me he could write care of the Queen Anne Hotel, or better still, he could come and visit me. And I had a strong feeling that he would.

On Easter Sunday, which was late that year, I asked her if she had booked for a holiday, and she said no. I said that if she left it any later she wouldn't be able to get in anywhere, and she came out with the usual: 'Who knows if I'll be alive?'

A few days later it occurred to me that this wasn't only talk. She meant it. Her bedroom, which was one of the biggest rooms in the house, was on the first floor. Normally she would be able to make it on her sticks all the way up to the landing without stopping for breath. Now I noticed that she had to stop at every step or two and I suggested she should have a room made up on the ground floor.

77

'On the ground floor? I'd rather be dead first.'

'You will be if you go on like this.'

'That's been my bedroom since the day I married. I have never really been able to sleep well anywhere else. Even during the air raids I would never go down to the shelter. If I have to die,' she said, 'I'd rather die in bed. And then there's all the things I have up there, the pictures, the bits of furniture, they mean everything in the world to me.'

'If you move them all down to the ground floor, it'll feel just the same.'

'I don't feel safe on the ground floor.'

'Nobody's going to steal you, you know.'

But she wouldn't listen, and, as if to show that there was life in the old bitch yet, she'd stomp up the stairs at the double whenever she thought I was watching.

One day I received a letter. It was typed and in a brown official-looking envelope. I knew without opening it that it was about my brother, Arthur. It was probably to say that he was in prison, which, on balance, would have been good news, or that he was in hospital and wanted to see me, and I told myself that if he was he could keep on wanting, and that if I did go to see him I would put a pillow over his face and put an end to him. I was certain of one thing: whatever was inside would upset me. As it was a bright morning and I was feeling good I left it unopened, but it wouldn't let me rest. I toyed with the idea of burning the letter without reading it, but finally after lunch I tore it open. It was about Arthur all right. He was dead.

At first I was irritated more than anything else. I thought he had done it deliberately to upset me.

I couldn't believe what happened next. Neither could the Old Woman. I sank down and cried and nothing she, or I, or anyone else could do could stop the tears. She made me a cup of tea, but I couldn't touch it. She poured me a glass of sherry, but I wouldn't have it. She 'phoned Ritchie and he came round with a whole pint of Guinness, but it made me cry even more. I couldn't speak to anyone so she did all the 'phoning for me. His body was in the morgue of a London hospital. She dressed, put her fur on and asked Ritchie to drive us there. He was laid out on a slab under a sheet. His face had been scrubbed clean, and his hair was neatly brushed, though he looked as if he could have done with a shave. His face had been lined and creased when I last saw him and it seemed to have straightened itself out. He looked younger, and I thought I could recognize the youngster who had run away from home. He'd done nothing with his life. Here he was, the boy who father hoped would be Station Master at Paddington, with gold braid on his cap, cold and dead as the slab he lay on. All I could remember as he lay there was the night I chased him and his woman out into the rain, and I broke down again.

They asked me what I wanted done with the body, and I said I wanted it buried beside my mother and sister Doris.

'That'll cost a fortune,' said the Old Woman in an awed whisper, 'hundreds.'

'I don't care, I want him to feel he's come home.'

'Hundreds,' the Old Woman repeated. 'You haven't got that sort of money.'

It took a bit of arranging but the Old Woman got Coggeshall to do it for me; Stanley, who looked as if he could be the Angel of Death himself, travelled down with the body by train.

To my surprise there was quite a turnout for the funeral, people who had known my parents or Doris, and who even remembered Arthur and me. Once it was over and he was in the ground, I felt a little better.

A woman whose brother had been Arthur's best friend made us a funeral tea. Her family used to be one of the poorest in the town, and I remembered her brothers as young ruffians who used to run in tatters and join Arthur in his raids on Woolworths, but she had a lovely house, with thick carpets and comfortable furniture and her tea was as good as a three-course meal. I remembered most of the names of the people there, but recognized few of the faces, not only because it was maybe thirty years since I'd seen them, but because they all looked so prosperous and well-fed, in well-cut coats and with matching handbags and gloves, so that the Old Woman in her moth-eaten fur looked like one of the poor relatives. I don't know what I could have looked like. I wore my funeral coat, a

79

black coat of Doris's which had been fashionable in its time and which used to fit me snugly. It now felt several sizes too big. I must have been losing weight.

We had been one of the better off families in the district and here were people who still remembered mother as 'a lady', which she was, if rather a poorly one, and Doris as 'a queen'.

'She looked like Moira Shearer,' said one woman.

'No, not Moira Shearer,' said another. 'Everyone said she looked like that oomph girl, what do you call her?'

'The oomph girl?'

'Yes, you know who I mean.'

'Anne Sheridan,' said somebody else.

'That's it, Anne Sheridan. All the boys were crazy about her. She'd have been a film star, she would, if she'd lived. But you're looking fine yourself, Phyllis, I must say, you haven't changed a bit. Looking at you I can see your mother.'

'I can see your dad, he was a nice man. Remember him in his uniform and the gold braid?'

'Best kept station in England.'

'But the trains spoilt it, at least during the war.'

'You're just like him, Phyllis. Haven't changed a bit, not in all those years. And slim as ever. Don't know how you do it. Look at me, been starving myself, and the kids still call me the old cow. We're going away this summer, to Greece, and I promised myself I'm not touching nothing – only sunshine. I'm going to lose twenty pounds if it kills me.'

'Doris was very slim, wasn't she?'

'No, not all over, she had it where she needed it. Of course that sort of thing wasn't fashionable till what-do-you-call her came along, you know, the "Outlaw" woman.'

'Jane Russell, but fashionable or not, she looked good. She could have been a film star. It was a shame her going so early.'

'My sister went at thirty.'

'Mine wasn't even thirty, a picture of health. You wouldn't have guessed there was anything wrong with her.'

'But you're looking well, Phyllis, haven't changed a bit,

not in all those years, don't know how you do it.'

'She was like Moira Shearer, Doris.'

'Anne Sheridan.'

'I thought she was more like Dorothy Lamour.'

'She could have been a film star.'

'Best kept station in England. Remember the daffs?'

'No, it was the dahlias what I remember.'

'No, not dahlias. It was chrysanths.'

No one said a word about Arthur.

As we were driving home, the Old Woman said to me: 'You need a good holiday, where would you like to go?'

And without even thinking, I said 'Frinton.'

7

THERE WAS NO letter from him waiting for me, and he wasn't there, not in Frinton and certainly not in the hotel. Two or three of the regulars had passed on, and there was in fact only one male guest during the four weeks we were there, a very tall, very thin brigadier, who spoke in a faint, muffled voice, as if he had a pillow over his face, and who was being looked after by his sister. For the first week or so I had no one to talk to at all, except the Old Woman, but she never had any time for me when there was anyone else around – not that I had all that much to say to her at the best of times. In the second week, however, there was a newcomer called Avril, who was looking after a tiny, shaky woman who looked like a sparrow which had been got at by the cat. Avril had a sallow complexion and reddish hair. She would have been quite good looking if it wasn't for a sore at the side of her nose and ulcers on the edges of her mouth.

We became good friends, and one evening she asked me if I would like to go out 'for a bit of fun'.

'What sort of fun?'

'There's only one sort what counts, isn't there?'

I still was not sure what she meant, though off-hand I didn't think Frinton was a likely place to find it, for it was, and is, a quiet, genteel town, with no fish and chip shops and no Chinese take-aways, and no pubs either, so that if you wanted a drink you had to go to a hotel.

'Where are you thinking of going?' I asked.

'There's Clacton. It's just a few miles up the road, and I've got a car.'

'But what if the little old lady wakes up?'

'She won't, and I see to it that she doesn't. She takes a pill to get to sleep, and I put another, sometimes two, with her drink, and she's dead until I wake her in the morning.'

'My Old Woman's not like that.'

'Can't you slip her something?'

'No, she'd smell a rat. Anyway, she likes me to be in bed early because she can't get to sleep till I come in.'

'You're entitled to a night off sometime. You can't be her servant day and night.'

That evening as the Old Woman was about to go to bed she turned and asked if I was coming with her.

'No,' I said, 'I'm going into Clacton.'

'At this hour of the night?'

'It's only nine.'

'But it'll be after eleven by the time you get back.'

'It might be after twelve, but I can't be your servant at all times of the day or night.'

'Who's asking you to be my servant? You don't have to do anything while you're here, a month's holiday and all found, but if you come in after I'm asleep I'll wake up again, you know I'm a slight sleeper.'

'Put a pillow over your head.'

'I'll still hear you.'

'Then put the mattress over your head.'

Avril was very nice. Since she thought the dress I'd put on was a bit large she took out a needle and thread to take it in. She also raised the hem a bit – too high for my tastes – so that my keees were showing, but she said that knees were an attraction and that I had nice knees. And all in a matter of minutes.

Then she sat me down in a chair, and gave me a hair-do. I couldn't remember ever having my hair done in my life. She made it stand on end slightly so that it added a good inch to my height, and finally she took off my glasses and made up my eyes.

'There,' she said, pulling me up to the mirror, 'how do you like that? I've made a new woman out of you.'

I couldn't see how I liked it because I didn't have my glasses on, but I felt a new woman and took her word for it.

It had been raining lightly in Frinton. It was raining heavily by the time we got to Clacton and she pulled at up a pub near the sea front.

Avril was quite a large woman, and her tight, red dress made her look that bit larger, especially in the bust. I had a Guinness and she had something from a small bottle with a gold-foil top. I wanted to pay for my own Guinness, but she treated me, and I was afraid that when she'd had her drink she'd expect me to treat her, but I couldn't, or at least, I wouldn't, not if she wanted something from a bottle with a gold-foil top. But it didn't come to that. The pub was packed and to judge from the loud laughter and the steamy faces most of the people around us had been there all evening. We hadn't been seated ten minutes when two men came over, large, cheerful-looking types with cigarettes in their faces and beer mugs in their hands.

'Does your mother know you're out?' said the first, which sent them both into fits of laughter, and I looked at Avril to see if there was some hidden meaning in what he'd said, but she wasn't amused either.

'Will you have the same again?' said the other.

'No,' said Avril, 'I think I'd rather have a gin and French.'

'Watch it,' said the first, 'she's expensive,' which brought on more laughter.

The second one went away to fetch a drink. He hadn't asked me what I wanted, perhaps because I hadn't finished my drink yet, so I quickly drained the glass and put it down loudly on the table, but nobody seemed to notice. I wasn't even sure if I really wanted another Guinness, but it would have been nice to be asked.

The two had, by now, introduced themselves as Sam and Syd. They spoke with thick Midlands accents and weren't well behaved. Sam placed himself on one side of Avril and Syd, on the other, somehow managed to keep his back to me all the time, which didn't bother me too much because his back was more pleasing than his front, but after about half-an-hour I'd had enough and said to Avril I was going home.

'It's early,' she said, 'we're having fun.' If this was her idea of fun, it wasn't mine, and I got up and said I'd take a bus.

'You won't get one at this time of the night, and you'll get soaked into the bargain. Have another drink.' And she turned to Sam. 'She'll have a Guinness.'

84

And Sam looked at me as if he'd seen me for the first time.

'So you're on Guinness, are you? You'd better watch it, or you'll get hair on your chest,' at which he and Syd almost choked with laughter, but he managed to gather himself together and came back with a whole pint of draught Guinness.

'She'll be running all night if she has that lot,' said Syd.

'Not if you fix her up with a stopper,' said Sam, and this time he actually fell off the bench with laughter and Avril helped to pick him up and dust him down.

'You're a crude lot you two,' she said, 'she's not that type.'

'Everybody's that type,' said Syd, 'unless they're past it.' And he turned to me. 'Are you past it?'

'No', said Sam, 'she's pissed it.' Now it was Syd's turn to fall off the bench, while Sam was caught up in a fit so loud and prolonged that the landlord came over and told him to watch it, which sobered them both up a bit.

'I don't like this place,' said Sam, 'they don't know how to treat a gentleman. Let's go to another.'

'Hardly worth it,' said Syd, 'they'll be closing soon.' And he turned to Avril.

'Can we got to your place?'

'No,' she said flatly, 'but what about yours?'

'Ours? There's my wife and kids there. We could try a beach shelter.'

'Not with me you can't,' said Avril, 'I'm a bit past that, but there's any number of hotels in the town.'

'A hotel?' said Sam. 'Do you know what a hotel would cost for the four of us? Forty quid.'

'Then go back to Birmingham, you mean buggers,' said Avril, and rose and strode out. For my part I wouldn't have minded trying a beach shelter, but it was too late for me to say anything – not that I would have said it. Sam, who looked as if he had a living ferret in his trousers, rose with difficulty and went after her. 'All right,' he shouted, 'have it your way, we'll go to a hotel.'

We went to a seedy little place in the next street. Avril and the men wanted what they called 'a night cap' in the bar before they went upstairs, but the Guinness was pressing heavily on me and I rushed into the powder room which happened to to be right next to the bar. Then as I was looking at myself in the mirror and thinking: 'Phyllis, what would Emily say to all this?' I could hear voices from next door. I wasn't sure which was Sam and which was Syd, for they were both alike and they were both shouting.

'You try her.'

'No, you can.'

'Me, I'd rather jam it in the door.'

'All right then, let's toss for it.'

'I've got a better idea, you have her, and I'll pay for the hotel.'

I didn't wait for more, but sneaked out on tiptoe into the street, and then walked through the rain to the bus station. There was no bus to Frinton, but there was quite a bit of traffic on the road. Doris used to travel everywhere by hitching. She only had to lift a finger and everything stopped. I tried to do the same, and some of the cars, and several of the lorries slowed down, but as I went towards them, they shot off, sending up spray on every side and covering me in mud.

I stopped under a tree for a minute, waiting for the rain to die down, but it became even heavier. I didn't mind getting wet, but I wanted to save something of my hair-do. On the other hand I didn't want to stop under the tree all night, so, rain or no rain, I walked on. It took about two hours to get back to the hotel. I was soaked to the skin and my hair was a mess of dripping tangles.

The next morning I came downstairs with an aching head, aching feet, a running nose and running eyes, but Avril looked even worse than I felt.

'Where the hell did you get to?' she said. 'We searched the whole place high and low. We thought you'd fallen into the loo or something.'

'I wanted to get back before it was too late.'

'You could have told us. Sydney was very disappointed.'

'Was he?'

'He thought you were a hot bit of goods.'

'That's why I went out, to cool down.'

'They'll be waiting for us tonight.'

'Not for me they won't. I'm going to bed as soon as supper's over.'

In the event she didn't go out either. As a matter of fact she went to bed after lunch and was still asleep in the evening, so I fed the little old bird of a lady for her and also put her to bed.

A few days later Avril asked: 'You're not staying in tonight, are you?'

'Why not?'

'It's Saturday, there's a lot happening on Saturday night.'

'If it's anything like what happened on Monday night, I'd rather stay in.'

'No, no, that was a mistake. Those two were a couple of creeps, and mean creeps at that. We'll go somewhere posh.'

'You mean expensive.'

'All right, so it might be, but I promise you, you won't have to buy yourself more than a drink, though you'll do me a favour if it's not Guinness.'

'What's wrong with Guinness?'

'There's nothing wrong with Guinness, but it's not what you'd call a lady's drink, not a proper lady's drink. Look, leave it to me, I'll get you something.'

I wasn't too happy with her idea. I had already left the Old Woman on her own one evening, and although she hadn't complained too much, I didn't want to make a habit of it, but Avril said: 'You can't be expected to stay in on Saturday night. Nobody stays in, not on a Saturday,' and she had the knack of getting her way. Besides, I hadn't been able to do anything with my hair since that night out, and I was hoping she'd fix it up again.

She fixed more than my hair.

The first thing she said was: 'You could do with a bit more out front.' She could have done with a bit less out back, but I said to her that was the way God had made me, and I was happy to stay as I was, and she said: 'Have you never worn falsies?'

'Worn what?'

And she took out a couple of things like the hollowed-out halves of a large grapefruit.

'What do I do with these?'

'Wear them you twit.'

I tried them on and I must say I liked the effect, but I wasn't very happy with them. It was a bit like cheating.

'What do you mean cheating? Are your teeth your own?'

'Yes, as a matter of fact.' She was surprised at that.

'Mine aren't. I've got three brothers and four sisters and we haven't a tooth between us. These things are just a bit of make up, that's all, but instead of doing up your face, you do up your body. You look good with them.'

She made up my face again and my hair, and again I felt like a new person, but a very self-conscious one, and though it was a warm evening, I insisted on wearing a raincoat.

'But you're spoiling the whole effect.'

'I'll take it off when we get to Clacton.'

We never did get to Clacton, or at least, I didn't, for as we were driving along, she said:

'These things are all right as long as you're fully covered, but when it gets to it, you've got to slip out quick and take them off – if you know what I mean.'

I thought I knew, but I didn't like the meaning of what I thought she meant.

'What sort of place are we going to?'

'What do you mean what sort of place? We're only going out for a drink.'

'Then why should I have to slip out and take them off?'

'Come off it, Phyllis, I know you're innocent, but you're not *that* innocent. One thing can lead to another. It wouldn't be worth dressing up and going out if it didn't. I don't have to tog myself up to the nines for a glass of Babycham. Don't you like a bit of the other?'

'I don't mind a bit, but I'm not going to start taking my clothes off, not at my age.'

'You sound like a virgin, you do.'

'I am a virgin.'

She braked and pulled into the side and looked at me with a mixture of pity and disbelief, as if I had told her that I was suffering from leprosy.

'That explains it. You're afraid of it, it's as simple as that.'
'I'm not afraid of it.'
'You're not?'
'No.'
'Has anyone ever laid a finger on you?'
'A finger? They've laid a whole hand.'
'And you're not afraid of going the whole way?'
'Not if it's with somebody I like.'
'Supposing it wasn't Cary Grant, would it still bother you?'
'No, not if I liked him.'
'You'd be surprised whom you can get to like when it comes to it.' And she drove off, a bit hesitantly, I thought, as if she was half-minded to turn back.
'Supposing . . .' I said.
'Supposing what?'
'Supposing we meet up with a chap who wants to take you out, but doesn't want to take me out?'
'It could happen. Nobody likes a prude.'
'Who's a prude?'
'You're a prude.'
'I'm a prude?'
'You said so yourself, you don't like to take your clothes off, and if that doesn't make you a prude you don't know what a prude is. Look Phyllis, I'd better take you back right now.'
'I don't want to be taken back.'
'You're going to cramp my style the way you're going on.'
'Why should I cramp your style?'
'If you're afraid of taking your clothes off, you're going to cramp my style.'
'In which case you'd better drop me.'
'You'll be sorry if I do.'
'I'll be sorrier if you don't.'
'A lovely evening like this, and you want to go back to the Queen Anne?'
'Well at least I won't have to take my clothes off.'
She stopped the car again.
'Look, do you want it, or don't you? It's the same with clothes on or clothes off, you know. The only reason for taking

your clothes off is that it saves them from getting messy and creased. And men can be very messy, at least if they're up to the job.'

'You'd better drop me,' I said, 'I'll take the bus back.'

'You're sure?'

'I'm sure.'

'I don't know how old you are, Phyl, but I'd say you were over twenty, and I don't know if you'll get a chance like this again.'

I had that very thought in mind myself, but all I could see ahead was another Sam and Syd, and I thought that if I could only learn about one of the great mysteries of life through them I would rather stay ignorant. Also the road was bumpy and the rubber grapefruit she'd lent me had slipped and were sticking out around my waist.

'No,' I said, 'I'd rather go back.'

'Scaredie.' I got out and she drove off in something of a temper. I suppose I was to her what Emily had been to me.

She called me on the house 'phone next morning. Her voice was croaky and hoarse and she didn't sound like herself and asked if I could give her little sparrow breakfast. She called me again at lunch-time to ask me to give her lunch. She came down towards the evening. She had her front teeth missing and a black eye.

She and the sparrow left at the end of the week, but before she drove off she kissed me and took my address and promised to write regularly, but I didn't think she ever would. And she never did.

8

ONE OF THE reasons why the Old Woman liked to go away in the summer was the thought of the pile of letters which would be waiting for her when she got back. It was never a particularly large pile, and most of the letters were bills, but there was nearly always something of interest – an open day, a memorial service, an anniversary celebration, a charity bazaar, a stone-setting, a consecration, a reunion – something to mark in her diary before Christmas. She could tell from the size and shape of the envelopes, and their colour, which carried the good news and which the bad. The bad news came in buff envelopes, the good news came in white, or in cream.

That year there was only one 'good news' envelope, an invitation to the centenary celebrations of her old school. It was not due until October, but from that day until then, she hardly talked about anything else.

'Wait till you see it Phyllis, it's a marvellous place, one of the best schools in the country, in some ways – at least in the ways that count – the best. It wasn't one of those crammers which tried to push obscure bits of knowledge down girls' throats, as if nothing else counted. As our headmistress – we called her the Beacon because her nose was rather red – used to say: "You come here not only be be educated, you are here first and foremost to confirm your heritage as ladies." I wouldn't say every girl that came was of good family. Some were merely from rich families, Jews and the like, but by the time they left they all behaved like ladies, which is my idea of a good school.'

The first thing she did was to 'phone her dressmaker who had made her last dress, but as she had not had a dress made in about twenty years I wasn't surprised to hear that the poor woman was dead.

'Why don't you go to the shops and buy a dress like everyone else?' I asked.

'That's something I've never done. I like to be comfortable in the things I wear, and besides I should like something special.'

She 'phoned around to see if anyone could recommend another dressmaker, but her likely contacts were also dead, or could not in fact suggest anyone, unless they wanted to keep the names to themselves.

She tried Crossleys for 'something elegant but practical', as she put it. They showed her something elegant, but when she saw the price she thought it wasn't practical.

'I furnished my house on less than that.'

We then went to London to a place in Kensington which seemed to specialize in outfits for ladies of her age, shape and handicaps. The carpets were worn out from the stomp of walking sticks and the tread of wheelchairs, and so were the shop assistants, frail, white-haired little women, bristling with pin cushions. There wasn't a customer who didn't want something taken in, or taken out, or raised or lowered, and the Old Woman was no exception, except that the others asked for alterations after they had bought their goods, while the Old Woman expected them before and I tried to pretend that I wasn't with her, which is something that happened almost every time we went shopping in London. She came away with aching feet, empty hands and a flaming temper, as if it was all my fault.

'I don't know why I keep coming up to London, it's a waste of time and money.'

'I told you that.'

'When did you tell me that?'

'Before you left.'

'By then I had already made plans to go, and when I make plans I like to stick to them. I'm not one of your flibberty gibbets who keep changing their minds all the time.'

When she calmed down I said to her:

92

'You've got a cupboardful of dresses you hardly ever wear, why don't you try one of those?' Which is eventually what she did. She put on a velvety thing in russet brown, with beaded bodice. She must have been a good bit smaller when she had it made. It was skin tight and the beads stood out on her torso like sweat. She also sent off her fur to be cleaned. I don't know what they did to it, but it came back with its hairs standing on end and when she put it on she looked as if she was in shock. She also bought herself a new handbag and gloves and even new unmentionables.

Finally the great day arrived, but she almost didn't, for old Ritchie did the usual and broke down.

Every time that happened she promised herself she'd get somebody else to drive her, until she found out what somebody else would charge, and so she went back to Ritchie. But we were lucky. An old lady in something very large and powerful pulled up. She was also on the way to the school, and gave us a lift.

The first person we saw was Mildred, who must have sent her fur to the same cleaner. As soon as they recognized each other they turned their backs on one another and looked like a pair of angry porcupines.

We were among the first arrivals. Most of the old girls who turned up seemed to be very old girls and five or six were in wheelchairs.

The Old Woman didn't use her chair. In fact she didn't even bring it with her, and hobbled around on her sticks for the whole afternoon, turning this way and that, looking for familiar faces. Every now and again she would stop some old dear, or some old dear would stop her with: 'You wouldn't by any chance be Victoria Fitzroy-Plunket?' or some such name, but she wasn't the person they thought she was, and they weren't the people she thought they were. Her sister seemed to be doing the same thing, but the more they looked the more they kept bumping into each other. She once mentioned that her sister was older than her, but she in fact looked younger. She was certainly less doddery. She sometimes smiled at me, but I was afraid to smile back. The Old Woman threatened me

93

with the direst things ten times a day, though it was so much wind in the chimney as far as I was concerned, but if she should have thought that I had any sort of friendly feelings towards her sister she would have sacked me on the spot. In fact I didn't feel one way or the other about Mildred, but I couldn't help thinking that anyone who was so hated by the Old Woman must have something to be said for her.

The Old Woman didn't even like me to mention her name, but once after she'd asked me how I got on with my sister, I took the opportunity to ask why she had fallen out with Mildred and she said:

'Quite simply because she's a monster who took advantage of me. It happened once. It happened twice. You may be sure that it will not happen a third time,' but she could not be drawn on what exactly had happened.

There was a service of thanksgiving, followed by a reception in the school hall in which they served a sickly sweet sherry which tasted like cough mixture, and salted peanuts. The Old Woman didn't like me to be too close to her when she was in company. I suppose she thought I cramped her style so I stayed by the table munching peanuts, until a small, squat woman with thick glasses and large teeth tapped me on the arm and said: 'You don't recognize me, do you?'

'No,' I said, 'I don't.'

'Nobody does, but I was watching you from a distance, and I recognized you right away. Do you know what gave you away? Your habit of pushing your glasses back up your nose.' She lowered her voice, and looked about her: 'You're Pippa, aren't you? I must say, I do admire your nerve in showing your face here. Remember *A Midsummer Night's Dream,* June 1925? You were Peaseblossom, and who was dear little Cobweb – in the shrubbery, during rehearsals? Remember? I thought you would.'

I would have liked to know more about Pippa, but I saw the Old Woman beckoning to me and had to excuse myself.

The school was divided into eight huge houses grouped in a crescent on the edge of the playing fields. She wanted to show me her house, and dragged me across the fields into one of the

94

buildings which had an odd smell of watery, slightly gone-off chicken soup lingering about the hall, then up the stairs, across a landing and into one of the dormitories. Sticks or no sticks, she could move faster than me if she got excited about something.

The dormitory, a long, narrow room, with two long rows of iron beds, was very sparsely furnished, like an old workhouse ward, but she stood there taking it all in with glowing eyes which almost lit up the gathering darkness.

'The fun we had after lights-out, telling stories – ghost stories – secret feasts and all under the blankets. The house mistress had a wooden leg and you could hear the hollow thump miles away. I slept here in the corner. Christine was here and Emily there, and then Stephanie and Victoria. I remember them all as if it was yesterday. What could have happened to them all? They couldn't all be dead.'

'They could, if they were your age.'

'What fun we had, what fun. There was an Indian girl, the daughter of a Rajah, black as coal. You just couldn't see her at all in the darkness. She'd creep around like a cat and frighten the life out of us. And there was another who was brown rather than black – I don't think her people were anything in particular – who complained of the cold all the time, and couldn't touch the food – for religious reasons, I think – and who cried herself to sleep every night. She did put a damper on things, but the other girls were a jolly lot, and as soon as she was out of the room we'd slip all sorts of things into her bed, mice, frogs, hedgehogs, even a dead cat once. She left after a bit. In an odd way we missed her.'

She steadied herself with a hand on one of the beds and began singing in a deep, breathless voice:

'None can deride,
Olde England's pride . . .'

I recognized the school song which she often hummed to herself, but this time she sang it right through from beginning to end, verse after verse. Her voice seemed to fade as she went on, and by the last verse she was sighing rather than singing.

'I don't know what people who haven't been to public school do for memories,' she said.

By the time we came downstairs the party was over. A thick mist had sprung up and men in heavy coats with turned up collars and large torches were directing cars out of the car park.

The old lady who had brought us to the school was kind enough to offer us a lift back. As we were moving into the drive, I thought I could recognize one of the car park attendants, but too late. The woman stepped on to the accelerator and he faded into the darkness.

The two women kept yattering about the old days, about Miss this and Mrs that, and the Bat, and the Frog and the Giraffe, which made the place sound like a menagerie, but I was hardly taking a word in. I could have been imagining things, especially in that mist, but I was almost certain that car park attendant was Walter. I had only seen his face for a split second in the torch light, but I had recognized his tall figure and hunched back.

On the way home we came upon poor old Ritchie who was still struggling to bring his car back to life, so we gave him a tow.

It was icy by the time we got back. It had been mild when we left in the morning, and I had left the heating off, so that the house was like a cellar. I don't think the Old Woman had got much joy out of the whole outing, and now she turned on me:

'Who asked you to turn the heating off? Don't you know it gets cold at night? Do you want me to die of pneumonia?'

'I was only trying to save you money.'

'Nobody asked you to. You turn the heating on and keep it on until I tell you to turn it off.'

I suggested she might feel a little better if she had a hot meal, but she didn't want that either, and I think she went to bed in her fur coat.

I couldn't get Walter out of my mind, and the more I thought about that stooping figure in the car park, the more I was convinced it was him. I wondered if I could take an afternoon off sometime and go up to the school and see for myself, but I had a better idea and sat down and wrote a letter:

Dear Walter,
    Am I imagining it, or did I see you working in the car park at Tennant's school?
    The school's not far from Crumpshall – about twenty miles – and a bus from here stops at the village about half-a-mile from the school gate. I suppose it would take about an hour to get here. I don't know what free time you have, but would you like to come and visit us one afternoon?
                        Yours sincerely,
                        Phyllis
(We met in Frinton the summer before last, remember?)

When a week had passed and I'd had no reply I thought I must have imagined it, but one morning a letter arrived in a surprisingly neat hand:

Dear Phyllis,
    Your letter was a nice surprise. Yes I work here doing all sorts of odd jobs. I get Wednesday afternoon off, but my older sister's turned funny and she's in a hospital a good bit away. I go to see her on my free day and by the time I've come and gone, the day's over.
                        Yours sincerely,
                        Walter.

I asked the Old Woman why she didn't visit her old school more often seeing it brought her so many happy memories.
    'I'm not sure that they would welcome visitors all that often. There's speech day, but it's very boring and they always use it to ask old girls for more money, as if we hadn't paid enough when we were pupils, and there's the annual Carol Service.'
    'Why don't you go to that?'
    'It's in December, about the time I'm busy with my Christmas shopping and other things.'

97

'You're not going to London for your Christmas shopping this year, are you?'

'No, I suppose I've seen the last of London. Not that I'm all that sorry. I can hardly recognize the place any more. It's dirty, seedy and expensive and full of foreigners.'

'Then why can't we go the Carol Service instead?'

'It would be such an expense, and Ritchie can hardly move five yards without breaking down, and to be honest I was a little disappointed with my last visit.'

'But it was nice to see your old dormitory.'

'It was, wasn't it? What fun we had, what fun, especially after lights out. The house mistress had a wooden leg and . . .'

Finally we went, and as soon as she was seated in the chapel I nipped out to see if I could find Walter, and there he was, on a ladder, mending the roof guttering. He nearly fell down when he heard me call.

'You? I didn't know you was coming.'

'I didn't know myself, not for sure, until yesterday.'

'What did you come for?'

'The Carol Service.'

'The Carol Service? It's on right now, you'll be missing it all.'

'The Old Woman's in there. I've come to see you.'

'Specially?'

'Specially.'

His face broke into a wide grin.

'Look,' he said, 'me hands is dirty. I'm going for a wash, but I'll be out in five minutes, maybe in ten. Don't go away.'

When he returned he had not only washed, but changed and we went together for a walk across the playing fields.

'I never knew you had a sister,' I said.

'Oh yes, I've had one for years. I went to stay with her for a bit after the Admiral died. Once, I was getting undressed for bed when I heard shouting downstairs so I rushed down in my bare feet, thinking she was being attacked or something, but she was there on her own, and raving at the top of her voice, and I didn't know if she had gone funny or I had, because there wasn't anyone there, or at least not that I could see. She

98

stopped after a bit, and said to me, "Well, that's put him in his place, hasn't it?" "Yes," I said, "it has," though I didn't know what she was talking about. A couple of days later we was having supper and I was sippin' me soup and she was sippin' her soup, when she looks up and shouts: "Who asked you to come here?" At first I think she's talking to me, then I see it's to somebody by the door who's not there, or who maybe is there, only I can't see him, and she turns to me and says: "Walter, tell him to go away." "Go away," I said, "go on, we don't want you here." Well, this goes on for about a week and by the time it's over I'm beginning to see the man himself and I ask her what she has against him. "He's pestering me, that's all. Some men take no for an answer, he doesn't." Well, I'm to start a new job in another few days and I don't know what to do so I go to the doctor and he asks if she ever got violent, and I said, no, not while I'm around. "That's all right then," he says, "people on their own get that way." Can I leave her then? "Yes," he says, "she'll come to no harm." A few months later I come to see her at Christmas and she's not there. She was found wandering in the streets in her nighty and they took her into hospital. She's been there ever since.'

By way of exchange I told him about Arthur, then he told me about his family, and I told him about mine. His story wasn't much happier. His parents didn't care for him, so he was more or less brought up by his sister. She was twelve years older than him and he was six or seven before it dawned on him that she was only his sister. He had thought she was his mother.

'I thought mother was a witch,' he said with a giggle. 'Sat by the fire most of the time with her hair bedraggled doing nothing much. She was past forty before I was born. She didn't know I was on the way, and thought she'd been putting on weight. She was put out when I turned up. My sister says if it wasn't for her she'd have flushed me down the lav.'

It was getting dark and misty, and from the distance I could see the doors of the chapel open and people filing out. I had to get back to the Old woman.

'Will you write to me?' I said.

'It's not easy writing.'

'But you've got such a nice neat hand.'

He hesitated for a moment, then he said:

'Well no, no, the cook did that for me. She also read your letter out.'

'Can't you write at all?'

'No, nor read – I can draw a bit though.'

'All right then, I'll send you addressed envelopes and all you have to do is to put drawings in them and send them back.'

'You want me to send you drawings?'

'Yes.'

'Oh, all right, if you want, but be careful what you put in your letters, she's a bit of a gossip the cook. It's all over the school, your letter.'

'Is there anything wrong with that? There was nothing really personal in it.'

'No, no, but she keeps nudging me and saying, "Who's your fancy woman then?"'

'Perhaps she fancies you herself?'

'Oh no, no, she's married you see, which doesn't stop her carrying on with the kitchen porter, though. It's him who spreads everything round the school. Everything she knows, he knows.'

'Look if writing's awkward, perhaps you can 'phone me? Can you read numbers?'

'Oh yes, I can read numbers.'

I gave him my number, and then reached up on tiptoe and kissed him on the cheek. He stood there like a statue with hands by his side.

'Aren't you going to kiss me back?'

'Kiss you back?'

'Have you never kissed a woman before?'

'No, not that I can remember, but I'll kiss you if you want me to,' which he did, on the forehead.

'You'll 'phone me?'

'I'll 'phone you.'

'Promise?'

'Promise.'

And I rushed across the fields to the car park.

Ritchie had got himself a new car, or rather a new second-hand car, and he complained about the mud on my boots. So did the Old Woman.

'People who can't keep their feet clean should travel by bus,' she muttered. She also complained that the school choir couldn't sing, that they had sung carols she had never heard of, and had sung them out of key and, worst of all, that the chapel was unheated and that she was sickening for a cold. 'I'll probably catch penumonia and it'll be your fault.'

9

FOR A DAY or two I half thought of asking her whether Walter could spend Christmas with us. We had never had a man staying over before (at least not that she knew of) and I couldn't see her saying yes to someone like Walter sleeping in one of her beds because, apart from anything else, he looked messy, but there were always things going wrong about the house, taps dripping, lights failing, windows cracking, frames breaking, chairs falling apart, and it was getting more and more difficult to find men to put things right, and when they did they charged a fortune. Old Ritchie used to help us out if we were stuck, but he was too busy now that he had his new car, and in any case round Christmas he never had any time at all. I could have put it to her that I knew someone who could do all the jobs that needed doing and he would do them for nothing, but they would take time, and we would have to give him board and lodgings for a day or two. I wasn't sure she would agree even then. I waited to hear from Walter before I said anything to her.

The 'phone didn't go often, but every time it went I dived on it. Sometimes I thought it had gone even when it hadn't, or if a whole day passed without it going once I'd pick up the receiver to see if it was still working. Some nights I woke in my sleep with the 'phone ringing in my ears, but it was only a dream. This went on for two weeks and when Christmas eve came and I still hadn't heard from him, and hadn't even received as much as a Christmas card, I did my best to forget about him. He had married once, it hadn't worked, and he was afraid to try again. Once bitten, twice shy. Or perhaps I had been too forward, writing to him out of the blue, pressing my 'phone

102

number on him, but whatever it was, he wasn't interested. It was nice to have someone to think about, but if he wasn't interested, then there was no use thinking about him and I was wasting my time.

Walter not 'phoning or writing was bad enough, but the thought of having to spend Christmas alone with the Old Woman was in some ways even worse, so I asked if I could invite Emily for Christmas (I don't even know why I asked because I couldn't imagine her leaving Bertha on her own, and I certainly wouldn't have wanted her to bring her with).

'Emily?' she said, 'Veronica's girl? Have you forgotten what it was like having her here last winter? It was the longest winter of my life.'

'She was only here five weeks.'

'They seemed like five years. She would exhaust the charity of a saint. Before she came here I hadn't realized how insufferable virtue can be.'

I half thought of 'phoning Coggeshall up and putting it to him that it wouldn't be a bad thing if he invited the Old Woman to spend Christmas with them. He had made her that party when she was seventy, which was about ten years ago, but she hadn't set foot in his house since, while she dined and wined him almost every time he was here, and spoke of him not only as her dearest friend, but as a member of the family (so was her sister, but there are members of the family and members of the family), but I didn't 'phone because until the last moment I was still hoping – hoping? I was sure – I would hear from Walter.

The Old Woman could see that something was happening, or rather, that something wasn't, but was nervous of putting a direct question. Instead she said to me: 'You look a bit down in the mouth', and I replied: 'You hardly look up in the mouth yourself.' And she wasn't. Up to the last minute she was hoping that someone would ask her for Christmas, and every time the 'phone went I could see her thinking: 'Ah, this is it', but she didn't get the call she was waiting for, any more than I did. Since the number of Christmas cards on her cord was now down to thirteen I stopped her from fretting about the unlucky number by buying a card so as to bring the total up to fourteen, but arrange them as she might they were still very few, and they didn't make an impressive display. Not only were her social acquaintances dropping away, but even the tradesmen.

To cheer her up I told her that the vicar had invited us for Christmas dinner, which wasn't true, and she said: 'Christmas day in the workhouse? You can go if you like, but not for me, thank you.'

Once we saw we would be on our own we did our best to brighten up the house, with a Christmas tree (a small one) and bits of holly all over the place, candles on the table and even a sprig of mistletoe over one of the lamps. I helped her into her corset, and she put on her black velvet dress with its lace collar and a string of pearls (real ones I think, but I wouldn't have known the difference if they weren't). All she needed was a little lace cap and she'd have looked like an over-blown Queen Victoria. I also put on my fancy best, which wasn't fancy enough for her.

'What's wrong with it?' I asked.

'Nothing, but . . . well, it's big for you. Don't you ever buy yourself anything new?'

'On what you pay me?' Which silenced her for a bit.

She dug into her drinks cupboard and brought out a fine display of bottles, all of which she kept at her end of the table, but she let me have a glass or two, or three. The table was long and I sat at one end and she at the other, but as the evening wore on she asked me to move closer, and began getting chummy.

'Tell me,' she said, 'why did you never marry?'

'I've had my chances, if that's what you mean.'

'I'm not saying you haven't, but if you have, why didn't you?'

'I had a sick mother to look after, didn't I? But if it comes to that, why didn't you remarry?'

'Oh, I could have done, times innumerable, but I couldn't – Edgar wouldn't have liked it.'

'Edgar?' I said, 'are you talking about your husband?'

'Who else?'

'But he's been dead nearly forty years.'

'And we were only married for twelve, but we were close, so close, and he was such a wonderful man. A gentleman, and I mean a real one. Nowadays people are so gruff and uncouth that anyone who takes his hat off to a lady is regarded as a Galahad, but he stood out as a gentleman even among gentlemen,' and, remembering what old Ritchie had told me about him, I almost blurted out: 'And what was he among ladies?' Did she not know, or had she forgotten and forgiven?

'I know you will think me a sentimental old fool,' she went on, 'but the dead sometimes mean more to me than the living.'

'Well, there's more of them for a start.'

'No, no, you misunderstand me. What I mean is, when people die they don't just vanish without trace, something of them remains. Don't you believe in ghosts?'

'I don't. Don't tell me you do.'

'I don't mean headless nuns and that sort of thing, but I do believe the dead are still with us. Sometimes when I sit up in the night I can feel them all around me.'

'Daft.'

'The trouble with you, Phyllis, is that you don't see beyond the obvious.'

'No, and I'd take something for it if I did.'

We had soup for the first course and turkey and trimmings for the next. As I was carving the bird, she said to me:

'You know, you wouldn't be too bad looking if you did something for yourself.'

'Such as what – have my face lifted?'

'No, but there's your hair for a start. Why do you leave it straight like that? Have you never used curlers?'

'What for?'

'Curly hair is nicer than straight.'

'Yours is curly, it hasn't done all that much for you.'

'My hair happens to be difficult to control.'

'My hair's been straight for the past fifty years, and it can stay straight for the next fifty. What's wrong with straight hair anyway?'

'Nothing at all, but some sorts of hair go better with some faces than others.'

'And what you're saying is that I should have kinky hair because I've got a kinky face.'

'I'm saying nothing of the sort. What's the matter with you? Can't I open my mouth in my own house?'

'No, but you don't have to get personal. I'll tell you something, if I had kinky hair like you, I'd have it straightened, like the blacks do.'

'I'm not going to speak to you any more.'

'Don't.'

'I won't.'

And she munched the turkey in silence, stopping every few minutes to pass some tit-bits to Rigby and Digby who were snuffling around on the floor looking like foot-warmers. She would slant her head as she was eating, now to this side, now to the other, just like her dogs, and wash it down with wine. Though she couldn't straighten her fingers, they were curved just at the right angle to fit over the bottles, otherwise I don't know what she'd have done, because she didn't trust me with the pouring. She did fill my glass every time she filled hers, but my glass was a tiny thing like an eye-bath, while hers held half a pint. I liked the sherry we had before the meal, but I didn't much like the wine we had with the meal and I said it had gone off.

'It hasn't gone off, it's a claret and a particularly good claret at that, but it's obviously wasted on you. Don't you know a good wine from a bad? You've been with me for goodness knows how long. Have you learnt nothing from me?'

'I hope I haven't.' I went on sipping the wine because I hated throwing anything out, but the fact is, claret or not, the stuff was like vinegar. She would take out a bottle whenever a visitor – which is to say, whenever Coggeshall – came. If Coggeshall finished it, good and well, if he didn't she kept the remains until the next time, and by the next time it was vinegar. I used to think it was meant to taste like that until I noticed that Coggeshall would put it aside and ask for water.

'It's the king of wines, claret. Father introduced me to it

when I was eighteen, and it's been my favourite since. He kept a splendid cellar. I wonder what happened to it? I still remember the dark passages and the bottles laden with dust. At Christmas there'd be five glasses to each table setting. I loved the hock glasses with their tall green stems, and their red cups, like tulips in bloom. Hock with the fish, you see. Then the hemispheres for claret. Many people prefer white wines with turkey, but father always had claret. He would have claret with almost anything. The third glass was for sauterne. He liked sauterne with the Christmas pudding and mince pies. And finally, of course, there were the liqueur glasses.'

'That only makes four. You said you had five.'

'That's true, I did. Now what *was* the fifth glass for?'

'Their teeth?'

Which brought her out of her reverie and I thought she was going to hit me with the bottle.

'You spoil everything. You're not fit company for Christmas. If I'd have known you'd be like this, I'd have made arrangements to be away. I shall next year. Some people become a bit more companionable after a few cups of wine. You merely become more offensive. You should stick to your Guinness.'

'I've had my Guinness.'

'Already?'

'At breakfast.'

'At breakfast?'

'I didn't have time to have anything else. I had to have this little lot ready, didn't I. Not that I get much thanks for it.'

'I have always appreciated your cooking.'

'You wouldn't think it listening to you.'

'I eat it, don't I, which is the most sincere form of appreciation. In any case, I have always remarked on the quality of your cooking, so has Mr Coggeshall, which is what made me ask why you never married? I had an uncle who married his housekeeper just because she was a good cook. Caused a scandal at the time, but in a way, I suppose, he had the right priorities. Some appetites last longer than others. Good cooks are always in demand, and there's no getting away from it, you are a good cook.'

'Thank you.'

'Mind you, it's not too difficult to be a good cook if you have good ingredients. I took great pains to find a choice turkey.'

'*You* did? You'd have bought a coil of old rope if I'd let you. It was me who picked it.'

'You did not.'

'I did.'

'You did not.'

'I did.'

'You picked something about the size of a sheep, and I said there's only the two of us and I don't want to be eating turkey until next Whitsun.'

'And you picked a scraggy little thing like a starved chicken.'

'That was for Rigby and Digby.'

'Rigby and Digby wouldn't have touched it.'

'This particular bird was picked by me. I saw it, I asked for it, I paid for it.'

'But only after I said I wasn't having the scraggy one.'

She drew her breath.

'I see it now. Remember I asked why you had never married? The answer is obvious. Because you always, *always* insist on having the last word. No man can take that, and frankly, I can't either.'

'All right, it's your bird. You not only saw it and picked it, you hatched it. Happy?'

'Have you ever, *ever* admitted that you were wrong?'

'Would it make you happy if I did?'

'It might.'

'All right, I was in the wrong. Don't ask me where, or when, but I was in the wrong. Is that better?'

'There you are, you see. You even apologize offensively.'

We ate quietly for a bit, though quietly is maybe not the word, because she had badly fitting dentures and was a noisy eater; also, her knife and fork, which she couldn't grasp properly, kept dropping with a clatter on to her plate or the floor (and I had to keep bending down to pick them up). I often thought of putting it to her that it would save us both a

108

lot of bother if we ate on the floor, or if she had the cutlery chained to the table.

At the end of the meal she poured herself a large brandy, and hesitated before pouring me a small one.

'I don't know if I should . . . it doesn't look to me as if you can hold it.'

'I can hold it better than you, and with half the practice.'

'I drink very moderately as a matter of fact.'

'Moderately? When I came back from Emily last Christmas I counted six bottles in the dustbin.'

'Is that any of your business?'

'I'm not saying it is, but you're trying to convince me you're a total abstainer, and I'm saying you're not.'

'I have a drop or two when I'm shaky.'

'You're shaky because you have had a drop or two. You don't need a wheel-chair, or even walking sticks, you need to sober up. There's nothing you can hide from me, you know, I'm not Coggeshall.'

'You're a wretched ingrate.'

'A wretched what?'

'Ingrate. You don't appreciate what I've done for you. I only took you in because the vicar told me it was my Christian duty.'

'And he told me I had to come here because it was *my* Christian duty. It's turned me off Christianity, being here.'

'Nobody's forcing you to stay, you know. I'm not as helpless as you think I am.'

'I'll bet you're not, not when you're sober.'

At which she turned, put the bottles one by one in the cabinet behind her, locked it, raised herself on her sticks and hobbled off without another word.

She had said that I could watch the colour television in her room over Christmas if I wanted, but after I'd cleared up I stayed downstairs in front of the old set. The screen was small, the picture wobbled and it always looked as if it was snowing, but I was used to it, and in any case they were showing an old film I had already seen three times so that I could tell what was happening without looking. I couldn't have been watching for more than ten minutes when I heard her bell going. I ignored it. It rang again, and I still ignored it. When it rang a third time I went to the bottom of the stairs and bawled at the top of my voice:

'Drop dead,' and with that it stopped.

I expected it would start again after a few minutes, but it didn't. When half an hour passed and she still didn't ring, I got a bit worried and went upstairs on tiptoe and put my head round the door. She was lying in a heap on the floor.

10

HER TEETH STOOD snarling at me from a glass by her bedside as if it was all my fault, which in a way it was. What she had said was right. I couldn't hold my drink and I might have had more than was good for either or us. We had our little quarrels every day, but it should have been different over Christmas, instead it was worse. I would stick to Guinness in future, and a little Guinness at that.

I 'phoned the hospital first thing in the morning and a nurse said she was 'as well as could be expected'. Since she could be dead and still be 'as well as could be expected,' I 'phoned again. They said she was alive, but could not receive visitors.

My next thought was to 'phone her sister. I knew that they had quarrelled but in such a situation quarrels shouldn't count, nonetheless it occurred to me that if the Old Woman came to and found Mildred by her bedside she might have a relapse, so I left it. I then tried getting hold of Coggeshall at his home address, but there was no reply.

There was nothing much else I could do now but wait, and as I didn't like waiting I started on the spring cleaning. It may have been a bit early for that, but she was always in the way when I wanted to do a proper cleaning job, and this was an opportunity I mightn't get again in a hurry. And in any case I like to be busy when I'm upset: it makes being upset less upsetting.

There was a small room at the very top of the house, which must have been the maid's room once, and I was on the floor scrubbing when I thought I heard the 'phone go. There was an extension in the Old Woman's bedroom and I rushed to answer, but by the time I got there the ringing had stopped. I had the feeling it was the hospital, and if it was the hospital they could have 'phoned for only one reason, so I 'phoned them back. The nurse I had spoken to before answered, with the same message – perhaps it was a recorded voice. Anyhow, I was satisfied on that score, but it left me wondering who the call could have been from.

Was it Walter? He had promised to 'phone, and he didn't seem the sort of man who would break a promise. He might have been busy with Christmas arrangements at the school and this was his first chance to speak to me. I left the attic and began working in the Old Woman's room to be near the 'phone in case it went again, but it didn't ring once and I finally tired of the silence and put on the radio for company.

Although I am quiet, I like to have someone around to talk to. By nightfall I was bursting to talk to someone, so I went and fetched my little note book where I kept all sorts of numbers and reminders and tried to 'phone Emily. There was no reply. I began talking to Rigby and Digby.

They had been in the bedroom when the Old Woman collapsed and were both left in a state of shock. When the ambulance came and took her away, I went back upstairs to put the room in order and found them both cowering in a corner, terrified that I'd do them in. When I brought up some food to show that I meant no harm, they drew back and still kept their distance. But their hunger got the better of them. They waddled towards the dish, sniffed it suspiciously, as if it was poisoned, and first one and then the other began digging in, and I had the feeling we were friends, which doesn't mean they were company, for they were both getting on in years, or perhaps they were just lazy. They came to life for a few minutes when there was food about, but otherwise they would fold their snouts into their flanks and drop off to sleep. If they didn't snore it would be hard to tell they were alive.

I switched on the television and, as the evening wore on, I found myself talking to the news reader. They seemed to have the same news every Christmas. The Archbishop of Canterbury making sermons here, the Pope making sermons

112

there, a snatch from the Queen's Christmas broadcast, ships in trouble off the Scottish coast. I suppose they had it all on film and used the same film every year. I was soon asleep.

The next morning I 'phoned the hospital. She was making progress but could still not receive visitors. I returned to the spring cleaning, with my ears cocked for the 'phone but it didn't ring (it never does when you're waiting). It was only then that it occurred to me that there was nothing to stop me from taking a bus down to the school to see Walter.

I washed, changed into my good shoes, put on my best coat, and even sprayed myself with the Old Woman's perfume and a couple of hours later I was at the school.

The place seemed deserted. If I had had a van I could have driven off with the chapel organ. There wasn't a soul around. Finally I knocked on the door of the gate lodge. The old man who came to the door said he had never heard of Walter. In fact he couldn't remember anyone of that name ever working in the school and he'd been there sixty years – though he was able to tell me where the cook lived.

She was a youngish woman, dark-haired, quite pretty and rather plump. She came to the door wiping her hands on her apron.

'I'm sorry to bother you,' I said, 'but I am told you're the cook.' She didn't seem to understand me.

'Cook?'

'The school cook.'

'Is a many cooks inna school.'

'But you may be able to help me. I am looking for Walter.'

'Walter?'

'Walter, the odd job man. Repairs.'

'You wanta repair water?'

I left it and finally managed to get hold of one of the porters who actually knew Walter. 'He was only temporary,' he said. 'Left just before Christmas.'

'You don't know where he went to?'

'No, but if you come back after the school holidays, the bursar might be able to help you.'

Then as an after thought I asked him about the cook, and

again I was told that there was a cook to each house.

'Yes, but there was one who was friendly with Walter.'

'Walter?' And he scratched his head. 'I suppose you must mean Stella, she's friendly with everyone.'

Stella was a large woman with a sweaty complexion and red cheeks, and when I mentioned my name something like a smirk spread over her face. I had found the right cook.

'He's not coming back, you know.'

'I know, but do you know where he's gone?'

'He used to see his sister every week, but they've let her out now and I don't know where he is.'

'Is there anyone around who might know?'

'There's nobody around. Come back after Christmas, the bursar might know, and even then I'm not sure if he will. Never said much about himself, Walter, at least not to me, he didn't. You'd think he'd have come in to say good-bye, because I helped him with one thing or another, but he didn't. One day he was here, the next he wasn't. He's like that.'

In spite of the disappointment and the expense I felt a little better for the outing, but darkness and gloom began to close in as soon as I was back in the house.

I tried to contact Coggeshall, but again there was no reply. I 'phoned Emily, and this time she answered.

'Funny you should ring now, I was just in the middle of writing to you. Did you have a nice Christmas?'

'It could have been worse, and you?'

'It started off very nicely. We were invited out by a friend of Bertha's, but something she ate must have disagreed with her, Bertha that is, for she was taken ill. She's still rather poorly, poor thing. I don't know what it could have been, because we all had the same meal, and none of us feel any the worse for it, but poor Bertha came out in spots and blotches and began feeling dizzy. But she's comfortable now, poor thing, which is something.'

'Look,' I said, 'why don't you come down to Crumpshall for a few days?'

'Oh I can't dear, I daren't, not while poor Bertha's poorly, and even if she gets better I don't know if I can afford the expense. Everything's so costly these days.'

I had forgotten that as Bertha's companion she wasn't getting paid at all, and I said I would write to her.

The next day the Old Woman was allowed visitors, and I came clutching a nice bunch of grapes and some flowers.

The ward was full of white-haired women of about her age, and it took me some time to pick her out, mainly because I was looking for a ruddy complexion when there wasn't one there. All the colour was gone from her face. Her cheeks, which used to be podgy and firm, were creased, and folds of flesh flopped loosely down the sides of her mouth. Her voice was weak:

'Are Rigby and Digby all right?' she asked.

'Yes,' I said, 'I've been looking after them.'

'You're not giving them tinned food?'

'No.'

'You promise?'

'I promise.'

Which seemed to satisfy her and she shut her eyes and dropped off to sleep.

She looked a good deal better the next day and her voice was much firmer.

'I see somebody brought me flowers and grapes, do you know who it was?'

'I did.'

'You did?'

'How did you pay for them?'

'How did you think I paid for them? Out of the house-keeping.'

'In future, before you buy me gifts with my own money, please let me know. Do you know what these things cost at this time of year? And in any case I never buy spring flowers before the turn of the year.'

I was glad to see that she hadn't changed and was making a full recovery.

I still couldn't get hold of Coggeshall but I did get hold of his secretary who said she'd send somebody down. He arrived that evening. It was old Stanley.

'What are *you* doing here?' I said, 'she's not dead.'

'But I heard she was poorly.'

'Yes, but not that poorly.'

'I thought I could be of help.'

'I don't know. If she sees you she'll think she's given up the ghost and have a relapse.'

I took him along to see her and to my surprise the sight of him cheered her up. It wouldn't have cheered me up. I don't know if he really was very old, but I thought of him as old. He was all in black, black coat, black scarf, black bowler, black-rimmed spectacles, black umbrella. Everything else was grey, grey moustache (which billowed as he spoke), grey face, grey hair. His nose was red, and that was the only colourful thing about him: and he had a slight stoop.

He walked me home from the hospital, which I thought was rather gallant of him because it took him out of his way.

'It's not safe for a woman to be out on her own these days,' he said.

'What? Even in Crumpshall?'

'Especially in Crumpshall, my dear. The quieter the place the more dangerous it is. Only last month something un-mentionable happened to a client of ours, a lady of nearly seventy, and in a quiet country town.'

I tried to get him to mention what the unmentionable thing was, but he wouldn't be drawn.

When we got home I thought he would turn for the station, but he obviously expected to be asked in for a cup of tea or something. I didn't mind getting him a cup of tea, or even something (though I thought he was past that), but I was afraid he might miss his last train and if the Old Woman heard that I had sheltered a man under her roof for a whole night, she wouldn't be too happy about it. Still if he wanted to come in I couldn't tell him to go.

'Would you like a cup of tea?' I enquired.

'That would be very nice,' and he took his hat and coat off. He seemed a bit lonely for company and someone to talk to, and once he started he didn't stop. He worshipped Coggeshall.

'A great man, but not very ambitious, you see. Looks after his clients as if they were his own family. He could have been

116

Lord Chancellor I think, or at least he could have been if he'd been a barrister instead of a solicitor.'

I asked him why he had never qualified as a solicitor himself, for he seemed to know a great deal about the law.

'Oh it wasn't so easy when I was a young man. I didn't come out of the army before I was thirty – I was a regular soldier, you see. Well, you're too old to start anything at that age, aren't you? I was lucky to get a job as a clerk, but I can't complain. At least I could, but it wouldn't be much help if I did.'

He looked much younger without his hat and coat, which is to say, instead of looking a hundred and twenty, he looked nearer seventy. At first I didn't pay too much attention to what he was saying because I was keeping an anxious eye on the clock, but as he went on it occurred to me it wouldn't be the end of the world if he missed his last train and I had to make up a bed for him. The Old Woman didn't have to know, and even if she found out she couldn't kill me for it. On the other hand she didn't care for hankey-pankey (at least if others were doing the hankey-pankeying) and she could make trouble for Stanley, not that there would necessarily be either hankey or pankey, for even if he did stay over we wouldn't have to sleep in the same room or even on the same floor, though given the sort of filthy imagination she had she would be absolutely convinced that we had been in the same bed, and as the night wore on I began to think that that was exactly what Stanley had in mind. And even if Stanley hadn't, I had. (Well, if you are going to be accused of doing something, you might as well go ahead and do it.) I didn't think I'd want him in my bed all night (I didn't think I would want *anybody* in my bed all night, because I value and enjoy my sleep), but if he happened to wander in from his room I wouldn't throw him out. He must have been quite a good looking man in his prime, and wouldn't be bad looking now if he shaved off his moustache. The more you got used to him the younger he looked. He said that he thought nothing of a twelve-mile walk, and sometimes walked as many as twenty, at a stretch. I didn't know too much about human anatomy, but I did reckon that a man who

117

could walk twenty miles at a stretch should be able to give a good account of himself in bed.

I had a couple of fancy nighties both of which had belonged to Doris – one of them so fancy, in fact, that I sometimes wondered what she had been up to – and I thought I'd better get into one of them (the less fancy one) as soon as I was upstairs. I'd also borrow a drop or two of the Old Woman's perfume (she'd never miss it).

I wondered if he'd ever been in bed with a woman. I'd heard of men who hadn't; I had even heard of men who didn't want to, and had met a few old men in my time who were really old women, but I didn't think Stanley was one of those. He was an old soldier, after all, but then he went on to tell me that he had been invalided out of the army after being wounded in action. I wondered where he had been wounded and, as I didn't want to waste my time, asked him outright.

'Oh, in the neck, you can still see the scar if I pull down my collar,' and he took off his tie, pulled down his collar and showed me.

'I was lucky. Another half inch and I'd have been paralysed from the head down, but as it is, there's nothing I couldn't do, even now.'

Well that settled that, but then, as I was wondering whether I shouldn't perhaps put on Doris's *other* nightie, he suddenly noticed the clock.

'My goodness, my train,' he said, and jumped to his feet.

He tried to 'phone for a taxi but couldn't get hold of one, and, grabbing his hat, coat and umbrella, rushed out into the night. I waited an hour or so, thinking he would be back for I was sure he'd miss the last train. Perhaps he did, and perhaps he walked back to London, but he didn't come back to me.

The next day when I went to see the Old Woman I found Coggeshall by her bed. He had just returned from an ocean cruise and was as black as a black.

As we were coming out of hospital he asked me if I had had any nursing experience.

'I nursed my mother for about twenty years. I don't know if that counts for anything. Why do you ask?'

'Because she's had a serious heart attack, and may need a nurse when she comes out. In fact she doesn't know it yet, but she may have to be moved into a nursing home. But there's one thing you can do right away. She can't use the upstairs rooms any more. Move her bed to the ground floor, and see to it that she doesn't use her sticks too much. If she has to move at all, she should use the wheelchair.'

The next day I got somebody in to dismantle her bed and bring all her things down from the main bedroom, shift the things from the front room and make it look as much like the bedroom as possible. I even changed the curtains round. Rigby and Digby kept shuffling up and down the stairs looking unhappy and bewildered, and I didn't think the Old Woman would be very happy about it either, but the word of Coggeshall was the word of law and I didn't think she would complain. And she didn't. But she complained about everything else.

'Terrible places, hospitals, they treat you like dirt,' by which she meant that they had treated her as just another patient.

'You saved yourself a few quid on the food,' I said.

'The food? It undermined my health. It was greasy and over-cooked, or greasy and under-cooked, but always greasy, and usually tasteless. It's a miracle one survives in these places. Next time I am taken ill I want to be left to die quietly in bed, instead of being poisoned slowly in hospital.'

She had been three weeks in hospital and had missed the Crossleys preview, which had also upset her.

'It'll be a year now before I see anyone I know,' she said. 'That's the terrible thing about being in hospital, it puts the time out of joint. You don't know if it's day or night, summer or winter. You should have told me about Crossleys.'

'A lot of good it would have done you if I had.'

'It might have helped to speed my recovery. It helps to have something to look forward to, otherwise there's no point of recovering. Did you go along at least?'

'Where to?'

'Crossleys.'

'What for?'

'So that you could have told people I'm in hospital. I never miss the sales normally. They'll probably think I'm dead.'

'Well they'll be half-right at least.'

Coggeshall came down the day after she got back and they were behind closed doors together for a long time, and I had the feeling they were talking about me.

If, as Coggeshall said, the Old Woman needed a trained nurse, then I wasn't up to it. I didn't know if she could afford to keep a nurse and me, but she grumbled about every penny she spent, and I couldn't see her laying out the money for both, and if she did get a nurse, I would have to go. But where? The second time I met Walter I wondered what I would do if he asked me to marry him. I couldn't see us both stopping under her roof and wondered what she would do without me, but I had a habit of worrying about problems which never arose. That problem didn't arise, and neither did this one. I don't know if Coggeshall told her that she would need a nurse, but she obviously didn't want one, probably because a nurse would have been more expensive than me and wouldn't have lasted.

The winter was mild, milder in fact than most of the summer, and after she had been back about a week she felt well enough for an airing. I helped her into her chair and we made our way to the park. The road was uphill and either she had put on weight, or I was out of practice, or both. The two dogs on her lap didn't make things easier and I had to keep stopping for breath every few yards. She got more impatient with every step and said: 'What's the matter? Running out of steam?' When I stopped yet again she lost her temper. 'It'll be dark by the time we get there if we go on at this rate. Can't you put your back into it?'

By the time she finished I was ready to put my boot into her.

The park was almost deserted. In mild days there were usually a number of other old crocks of her age around the park and she would give them a going over from a distance (with a pair of opera glasses she kept under her travel rug for the purpose) to see if they were 'people of quality' as they used to say. There were a couple of old men in wheelchairs, pushed by even older men, and none of them were her types.

'When I was a young woman,' she said, 'if you saw somebody in a wheelchair you would take it they were of good family, but now half the country's in wheelchairs. I'm not a snob, but if I find myself in conversation with people without education I have nothing to say. It was awful in hospital, I had no one to speak to at all. There were two old women, one on each side, both hard of hearing and both shouting to me – or perhaps they were shouting to each other – about holidays they had had on the Costa del this and the Costa del that. They used to say travel broadens the mind, but one has to have a mind in the first place. They've been everywhere, but don't know anything, except the price of getting there and back.'

She broke off to turn stiffly to see if I was still there.

'You're very quiet this morning,' she said.

'There's no point in my saying anything, is there? I ain't had no education.'

'But you've mixed with people who have, which also counts for something. It was dreadful in hospital, dreadful.'

'They got you back on your feet, didn't they, or at least back into your wheelchair.'

'The medical part of it was all right, but socially it was an ordeal. And the food wasn't anything special either, all starch, stodge and grease.'

'Why didn't you go into a private hospital?'

'A *private* hospital? Do you know what those places cost? I had a friend who went into a private clinic for a small operation. The operation was successful, but the cost killed her. In any case, why should I go into a private hospital? I pay enough in taxes to be entitled to a place in a public one.'

It started drizzling. I·got up and began to push her downhill.

'Where are you going?'

'Home.'

'Who said I wanted to go home?'

'It's raining.'

'It isn't raining, it's only drizzling. And in any case I'm not made of sugar.'

'You're only just out of hospital, you've got to watch it.'

121

'That's for me to say.'

We sat down and waited until the drizzle turned to rain, by which time it was too late to make a dash for home and we had to take shelter in a small pavilion near the bowling greens. Three old men, chatting in low voices, broke off when we entered. They looked at us and we looked at them and it took them a minute or two to get restarted.

'The worst thing wasn't the shelling,' said one in a low voice.

'If you can say that, you don't know what shelling is,' said another.

'I don't know what shelling is? Wasn't I on the Marne?'

'Yes, but was you right up front?'

'If you was in the battle you was in the battle back or front. The shells was bursting all over.'

'I can still hear them to this day.'

'But the worst thing was being wet.'

'Being wet? We was wet all the time.'

'Yes, but there's wet and wet. We was in two feet of water, right up to the waist.'

'If it was two feet it couldn't have gone up to your waist, not unless you was on your knees.'

'All right, we was in three feet of water. It was a lake. I remember one of me mates saying, it's not generals we need, it's an admiral.'

After about half an hour of that we thought we would be better off in the rain, and made a dash for home. It was downhill nearly all the way and she squealed with joy as we hurtled along. 'Faster,' she cried, 'faster.' And I went faster because I was being carried along by the chair but I hadn't got far before I slipped and she went hurtling downhill on her own. She couldn't have heard me cry out and she went on whooping as if she was playing Red Indians. I picked myself up, dashed after her and grabbed the chair just as it was about to go into the road. It hadn't occurred to me that I could move so fast.

'That was fun,' she said. 'Let's go uphill and then down again.'

'You're going home,' I said.

122

'Just once more.'

'You're going home,' and she knew me too well to argue.

When we got home I nearly collapsed and had to have a cup of tea before I could pull myself together, so that lunch was late, which upset her since she liked everything on time.

Towards evening she had a more serious upset. As it grew dark the temperature suddenly dropped and, as if to celebrate the onset of real winter, the central heating conked out. It was pretty late by the time we realized it because, even when the heating was going full blast, it wasn't all that warm and during the really cold weather the Old Woman would shuffle round in her fur or hug the radiator; but while she was settling down by the kitchen radiator she found that the heating wasn't on at all.

Since it was too late to 'phone the engineers she asked me to put on some electric heaters. I reminded her that the last time I did that the fuse blew.

'Are you suggesting that we sit here and freeze?'

'No, but you could go to bed and I could get the central heating man first thing in the morning.'

'He mightn't come for a week, and in any case I don't feel like going to bed.'

'You're usually in bed by this time.'

'Well I feel like staying up tonight, do you mind?'

'All right then, I'll put on the gas oven.'

'The gas oven? What good will that do?'

'Well you could put your head in it for a start.'

At which she got out of her chair and somehow plugged in one of the heaters herself. As she did so there was a flash, a scream and we were in darkness.

The next morning I had to search around for a central heating engineer and an electrician. I found an electrician, but the people who had put in our central heating were out of business (which didn't surprise me at all) and so I spent the better part of the day on the 'phone before I finally got hold of a plumber.

The electrician had the lights back on in a minute, but told us not to use the heaters because the whole house had to be rewired. 'It'll cost you thousands,' he said cheerfully. The Old

Woman wouldn't believe him, until he asked to be paid for the minute he was there, which was twelve pounds.

'That comes to over seven hundred pounds an hour, you can't be serious.'

But he was. We were terrified what the plumber would charge, for he and his mate had spent half the night with us, and he said he'd have to come back in the morning.

'I don't know who put your heating in,' he said, 'but he didn't know the first thing about it. You're lucky you didn't have an explosion.'

It took them nearly three days to put it right, and left us with a bill for three hundred pounds. She was struck dumb by the sight of it. Even I winced.

'I can't afford to live any more,' she said, 'that's the long and the short of it.'

11

THE OLD WOMAN had grumbled about money and the high price of everything for as long as I'd known her, but I took it that that was the way of the rich, for the Dragon too used to complain and she had left a fortune. Now I could see that she really had something to grumble about.

Prices had been rising for as long as I could remember, but that winter they began to go wild. In the past, by shopping around, I had managed to keep the larder full even though she had given me the same amount of housekeeping year after year. Then suddenly *everything* went up and there was nothing I could do but buy less. I had thought that all she had to do was to pull up a floor board, or something like that, and dig into her hoard and everything would be all right, only now I could feel that something had changed, and that her hoard – if she had ever had one – was gone.

She would be on the 'phone to Coggeshall in a wailing voice almost every day, and when Coggeshall came down for a meeting she no longer had her hair done, and she didn't even put on her dress with the beaded bodice or offer him a meal. She no longer brought out the wine for the Sunday lunch, for that would have meant giving me a drop (though if she thought I wasn't looking she would still help herself to a quick nip).

Then, one afternoon while she was sleeping, a man came to the door and said he was the architect. I said which architect, and he said: 'Chapman. Didn't Mr Coggeshall tell you? Weren't you expecting me?'

I woke the Old Woman, who was expecting him though she wasn't particularly pleased to see him (not that she's ever pleased to see anyone when she's roused from her slumbers).

He spent a couple of hours sniffing about the house, opening doors, poking his nose into crannies, making notes. When he was gone I asked her what it was about.

'It upsets me even to talk about it. It's Coggeshall's idea. He wants to convert the upstairs rooms into a separate, self-contained flat.'

'That's a good idea. You never use it. I could move downstairs.'

'They'll have to build another room and bathroom on the ground floor. I don't know where I'll put everything. I won't recognize the place by the time they're finished, and I won't have any room to put up friends or guests, but the worst of it all will be having a complete stranger right on top of me. Coggeshall put the idea to me ten years ago and I said "over my dead body," but I hardly have any option now, have I?' She was almost in tears.

Some weeks later the architect came round with some papers which she had to sign.

'It's like signing away my birthright,' she said 'and God knows what sort of people we may be having on top, but there's no alternative.' And she clasped the pen between her thumb and forefinger and put her name to it.

'We've got six months grace before the builders start work, so perhaps I'll die before it happens.'

'You'll be lucky.'

But the builders never got started. The house, apparently, was listed as a building of special architectural interest, so the local authority wouldn't accept the plans.

'We'll be able to revamp it here and there, move the stairs across and alter the dimensions of the exterior slightly. Shouldn't be too difficult to satisfy them,' said the architect.

'What? Deface a national monument?' she said, 'Never.' And she wouldn't let them touch a brick.

Coggeshall came down specially to 'confront her with reality,' as he put it, but she would not be moved.

'If I have to starve I shall starve, but I shall let no one touch this house.'

'You're not being very sensible, Martha.'

'I don't have to be sensible at my age.'

'You don't appear to realize what's happened to your shares.'

'I realize only too well, unfortunately, I'm not senile, but as long as I have breath in my body, this house stands as it is. I'll never forgive myself for having allowed the architect to set foot here in the first place.' She sounded like a woman who had been talked into being unfaithful to her husband, and could not forgive herself. 'I was married here, I was happy here, and I shall allow no stranger to set foot in it no matter how much they may pay, and no matter how much I may need their money.'

As she went on, Coggeshall grew redder and redder and I was afraid he might explode long before she was finished.

'Do you realize the cost of fuel has quadrupled?' he shouted. It was the first time I'd heard him raise his voice. It was high-pitched and he sounded like a woman. 'Do you know what it costs to heat this place? To keep it in decent repair? Look at it. The plaster is cracked, the paint is peeling. It could collapse on top of you.'

'It's still got another few years to go, which is more than I have.'

'I wouldn't be so sure. Your mother lived to be ninety-five.'

'She didn't have a heart attack.'

'Heart attacks are nothing these days. Everybody has them. I've had a heart attack, and the way you go on you'll be bringing on another. You're sitting on a fortune and you're letting it crumble into dust. I shan't allow it, do you hear? As your legal adviser, and trustee, I insist that we rebuild the house and I shall instruct the architect to present new plans forthwith.'

'You can do what you like, but I shan't sign the papers, and if a builder sets foot in this house I shall club him with his own bricks.'

'There's no point in talking to you now. You've obviously not quite recovered from your illness and don't realize the gravity of your situation. I shall return next week, by which time I hope you may have recovered the use of your senses.'

127

And he slammed his bowler on his head and strode out.

He did not return the following week and I had the feeling that he had washed his hands of her affairs. I suppose I would have done the same.

I tried to argue with her myself, but she wouldn't see reason. What had done the damage was the discovery that her house was of 'special architectural interest,' 'part of our national heritage,' as she put it, and in fact the way she went on about it you'd think it was Windsor Castle. She spent hours in the local library and discovered – or thought she had – that the house had once been owned by a titled family. I said to her: 'Why don't you open to to tourists on Sunday afternoons? You could make a few bob that way.' And she thought I was being serious.

In the meantime she began to cut down right and left. She cancelled the *Daily Telegraph* though when I told her that it would leave us without paper to line the dustbin she got the *Mail* instead. Our daily bottle of gold-top was changed to red top. She stopped making a weekly order at Crossleys and made it monthly instead, and she closed her account at Lamb's, and bought her meat at the supermarket instead where it was half the price. I was even more sorry about it than she was, for I liked to chat with Mr Lamb, or, if Lamb was away, with his assistant, a red-faced man with a filthy mind, who gave a smutty undertone to everything he said:

'There's a nice pork sausage – think what you could do with that.' Or: 'How would you like this between your chops?' The meat we got in the supermarket was just as good, but it meant one place less to stop on our morning walks and I was afraid that with no Lamb the next thing might be no Frinton. When Easter came and she had not mentioned holidays, I asked her if we would be going away at all.

'Depends what they charge, and what old Ritchie charges. Getting there is getting to be almost as expensive as staying there, and it's not all that cheap to stay. On the other hand I think we need a break, don't you? I still haven't got over that stay in hospital.'

Which cheered me up a bit. I had almost given up all thought of Walter, but I hoped I might see Avril. She was a bit coarse, Avril, but good fun. Where there was Frinton there was hope, and in fact she made her usual booking for the month of June.

Then Rigby was taken ill, or maybe it was Digby, because I was never sure which was which. Both had become stout, smelly and slow-moving, and were losing their hairs so that they began to look like elderly pigs, and in fact they were too heavy for the Old Woman to have on her lap, so that when I took her out for an airing in the chair I would have them both beside me on a lead, and once, as I was pushing her uphill, I lost my step, the chair moved back and went right over poor old Rigby (or was it Digby?) He gave a yelp which sent the Old Woman flying out of her chair, and I had to rush him to the vet, who sedated him (he should have sedated the Old Woman while he was at it), X-rayed and put him in plaster. It was three weeks before the poor beast was on his feet. The bill put the Old Woman on her back.

'Ruin, ruin,' she kept wailing. 'It's a conspiracy to rob me.' And, of course, she blamed everything on me and said I had run over the dog deliberately. It was something I might have done when he was younger, but as they grew older they looked so miserable and helpless that I didn't have the heart to kick them, even when she wasn't about, or maybe I was getting soft with old age.

'I've a good mind to stop the money out of your wages,' she shouted.

'You'd have to start paying me first wouldn't you?' I said, which shut her up for a while.

To avoid further accidents she decided that she couldn't have the dogs with her when she was in the chair, and, as they would pine if they were left on their own, she was never out for more than half-an-hour or forty minutes. And if we hadn't finished our morning's round of shopping in forty minutes, we would have to go back again in the afternoon. I don't know what happened, perhaps she thought the dogs needed a change, but one day she decided to treat them and herself (and me) to a run in the country. I was surprised at her extravagance but she said: 'Who knows how many more days

like this I shall have? Let's make hay while the sun shines.'
And I prepared a picnic lunch for us and the dogs, a thermos
of coffee and old Ritchie arrived to take us for a run to
Virginia Water.

'Now Ritchie,' said the Old Woman, 'I shall repeat my
warning. If this vehicle breaks down either before we get to
our destination, or on the way back, I shall not pay you. Is that
understood?'

'No, not this car, never had trouble with this car. Hasn't
broken down yet.'

Well, the car didn't break down, but old Ritchie did. We
were in a traffic jam at the time, but when the traffic began
moving we didn't.

It began to rain. Somebody called an ambulance. Somebody
else took us home. I put out our picnic on a tray and we sat
down to watch television. It was an old film with Rex
Harrison, her favourite actor, and she told me to take the
'phone off the hook because she wanted no interruption.

'The 'phone never goes in any case.'

'It does when I don't want it to.'

And at that moment, it did. It was to say that old Ritchie
was dead.

He was a dear old man, bald as an egg with broad shoulders,
short legs and no neck, and I was afraid with him gone there
would be no more outings to the outside world, no runs in the
country, no school reunions and, I was sure, no Frinton. I felt
everything closing in on us.

The Old Woman was very upset.

'I can't see the point of going on, I really can't. Everyone I
know, all the best people, are dead.'

To cheer herself up she started buying meat at Lamb's
again. 'He's about the last person left in the town that I still
know,' she said, but even if Lamb was hale and hearty, his
business was on its last legs, and a few weeks later it closed
down. 'The sort of people who appreciate personal service
can no longer afford it,' he said.

At that the Old Woman took herself to her bed. 'I don't
want to be disturbed,' she said, 'I just want to be left to die.' In

fact she spent most of the time watching television. I don't know what programmes she watched, but they left her in a foul temper.

One evening I made roast potatoes. Actually, I made them almost every evening because they were her favourite food, but this time she complained that I had taken all the brown potatoes and given her all the pale ones.

'Look,' I said 'yesterday you were complaining that I had taken all the soft potatoes and given you all the hard ones. So, this time I gave you all the softer ones.'

'They're not soft, they're half-baked, almost raw.'

'All right, have mine.'

'No thank you, not after you've mauled them.'

'I haven't touched them.'

'You've just dug your fork into one.'

'But I haven't dug my teeth into it.'

By the time she had finished I was ready to put my potatoes, and everything else on the plate, over her head.

She liked a fruit salad, but complained that I'd put more grapes in my salad than in hers, or that the cherry on top of my salad was larger than hers, and that her cherry had gone mouldy, and that in any case she didn't like glacé cherries. I was afraid that if we didn't get away in the summer, one of us would murder the other, and I knew who would be murdering whom.

And it looked as if we weren't going. I asked around the other car-hire companies how much they charged for a run to Frinton, and they were almost twice as expensive as Ritchie, and Ritchie, as she reminded me, hadn't been all that cheap.

'There's always the train,' I said.

'And travel in the guard's van with chickens and dogs? No thank you. I'd rather stay at home. Besides, the hotel rates have gone up again so we can't really afford to go.'

Then I had an idea.

Somebody told me about an organization calling itself 'Push Pals', or something like that, which had a special bus to take the physically handicapped on holiday outings. You had to be careful not to use the word 'handicapped' within the Old

131

Woman's hearing. She hated the word and she made it plain that she, for one, was no such thing. 'I may be crippled,' she said 'but not handicapped.' It so happened that this group was organizing a bus to Frinton from the first Sunday in June and every Sunday after that throughout the summer months.

When I told her about it, she said: 'I smell a rat. It's some sort of charity runabout organized by the vicar.'

'It's not charity, you pay.'

'How much?'

'They leave that to you.'

'In which case it's worse than charity. You pay through the nose and they still think they're doing you a favour,' but after grumbling on for half the morning she said she'd think about it, which was her way of saying yes. But when the day came, she took one look at her travel companions, and turned about.

'It's a poor-house outing,' she said in a loud whisper.

'They won't be at your hotel.'

'But I'll be with them all the way there in the bus. They look diseased.'

'They're getting on a bit, that's all.'

'Getting on? They're vegetables and rotting vegetables at that.'

'You're not in the first bloom of youth yourself, you know.'

'At least I'm continent.'

She reluctantly allowed herself to be pushed up the ramp and into the bus, but took a place right at the back with me beside her, held up her umbrella like a truncheon and looked as if she might attack the first person who tried to come near her.

It was a very long journey. The passengers were continent, but only just for we must have stopped at every public lavatory in the hundred miles between Crumpshall and Frinton. There were a number of young people on the bus. One of them had a guitar and they tried to entertain us with hymns and pop songs. The Old Woman complained that if they didn't stop right away she would have to be let off the bus, so they stopped. She then asked for the windows to be opened, and when they were opened she asked for them to be closed. I

132

tried to edge away, pretending that I wasn't with her. When we were about half way there one of the old men conked out, and we had to leave him at a hospital, which for some reason cheered her up a bit, but not for long. A pretty young woman with huge blue eyes, like saucers, came over and asked her if she wanted a drink.

'No,' she said, 'we're not thirsty.'

'But I am,' I said. 'Anyway you're supposed to be a lady, couldn't you have said no thank you?'

'I am a lady, and expect to be treated like one, which is why I said "no". I don't like charity – especially in plastic cups.'

Frinton was a disappointment. The weather was fine, the hotel was as comfortable as ever, and we were well looked after, but nearly all the guests were men and the pushers seemed more decrepit than the people they were pushing. For some reason I still thought that Walter might turn up, but there was no sign of him, and no sign of Avril either.

There was a woman there in an 'electric chair' (at least that's what she called it) with whom the Old Woman struck up something of a friendship.

'You must get yourself one,' she said, 'it's the greatest invention since steam. Before I got the chair I was at the mercy of my servants. They cheated and robbed me, and bullied me, and I had to await their pleasure before I could get out of the house. I had to provide them with their own room, and their own television, and special diets in some cases, and the wages they charged were extortionate. But worst of all, when you needed them, when you *really* needed them, they pretended to be deaf, or weren't there. I had a woman, a *respectable* middle-aged woman from a *respectable* middle-class family living in with me. As a matter of fact we were vaguely related. Last Christmas eve she said she had to pop out to visit a friend, and didn't come back till five days later, looking the worse for wear. I was all alone in the house, by myself, a prisoner. It was then that I decided to go electric, and I bless the day I did. You should do the same.'

'Aren't they expensive?'

'They are a bit, and you have to keep charging the batteries, but they pay for themselves a hundred times over. Here, try it.'

She did. It crawled along like a palsied snail, but she seemed to enjoy it and she watched to see if I was watching as she went forward, and reversed, and turned this way and that.

'They're marvellous,' she said. 'Almost like having your legs back. I think I'll get one.'

After that every time we fell out, which was about once every five minutes, she would threaten me with an electric chair.

The quarrels apart, it was a very dull holiday and I couldn't wait to get back to Crumpshall. The Old Woman had enjoyed her stay, but what put a damper on it was the thought of going back in that bus and I only discovered how much she really dreaded the journey when she put her hand in her pocket and hired a car instead.

'This may be my last journey,' she said.

When we got home there was such a pile of letters that it was difficult to push open the door. They were nearly all bills.

'My annual homecoming,' she said. 'They wait specially, so that even if you had enjoyed the holiday, they can ruin it for you. Look at them. Gas, water, electricity, oil, rates, repairs, maintenance. They must think I'm made of money. You know what I'm going to do? Burn them.' And she went to the kitchen, put all the bills in the sink, poured on paraffin, added a match and watched the fire with glowing eyes. There had been many times during the many years I was with her, when I'd wondered if she had a screw loose, but for the first time I was almost sure of it. She was going, or perhaps had gone, mad. I think it was the cost of hiring the car which had been the last straw. Her whole wedding trousseau, she told me, hadn't cost half as much.

12

ONE DAY I got a letter out of the blue.

Well, nearly all the letters I got were out of the blue. Emily was about the only person I ever heard from and she only wrote every five or six weeks. Then came this letter in a scrawly hand, which I could hardly read and, in fact, it looked as if a fly had fallen into an ink bottle and had crawled across a large sheet of paper, but I thought I could recognize the word Walter here and there and, gradually, with the help of a magnifying glass, I made out, or thought I made out, what it was saying.

The letter was from Walter's sister to say that he had left the school and was now working as a gardener in Dorset, and that he had tried to 'phone me a number of times over Christmas, and during the summer, when he was on holiday, but since there had been no reply he was wondering if I had moved. He was all right, and he was hoping that I was.

I at once sat down and wrote that I hadn't moved and was wondering why he hadn't 'phoned because I didn't think it was like him to break a promise, and then I decided that writing was an awkward way of saying something when he couldn't read, so I decided that the best thing I could do was to travel down to Dorset. But what could I do with the Old Woman? She could no longer be left on her own. It wasn't only that she couldn't get about, but I was almost sure that she had turned ga ga. I would sometimes hear her mumbling to herself, and once or twice I looked up from my porridge at breakfast to find her smiling. She was not a great smiler at the best of times (neither, for that matter, am I), but who smiles at breakfast? Once I even thought I could hear her singing, but what worried me most was her habit of turning on the gas and then, as she looked around for a match, turn to something else, so that more than once I rushed back from shopping to find the house full of fumes. It would take me the better part of a day to get to Dorset and back, and I was afraid that by the time I returned she'd have blown up the house and herself with it. There were times when I thought that mightn't be a bad thing, but I didn't want to have it on my conscience.

My first problem, therefore, was to find a stand-in, and I thought of 'phoning Emily, but I was sure the Old Woman wouldn't let her into the house so I had to think again. And it was then that I remembered Avril. She had her own old woman to look after, but she had a car and didn't live too far away. She could bring her over for the day. It was a bit much to ask, but I didn't often ask for favours and, if necessary, I would pay her, but I had to get to Dorset one way or the other.

I 'phoned Avril and at first she didn't remember who I was. 'Phyllis,' I said, 'Sam and Syd, Clacton, have you forgotten?'

'Oh yes, the falsies, I remember.'

When I explained the situation she was very understanding and offered to come down any time I liked.

I then had to tackle the Old Woman which was less easy. She first of all wanted to know where I had to go and why.

'It's a private matter.'

'Private? How private?'

'Very private.'

'In which case you'd better go. I daresay I should be able to cope on my own for a day.'

'No, no you won't have to. A friend of mine is coming over to . . .'

'A friend? Which friend? You don't mean the fat one?'

'No, no, Avril, she was in Frinton the summer before last, do you remember?'

'You mean with the painted hair?'

'Yes that's right, reddish hair.'

'And the tight dresses?'

'Tight dresses? Did she wear tight dresses?'

'Bulged on every side like an over-filled sack of potatoes. To be frank, I was surprised to see you two out together. I had the impression you were more discriminating than that.'

'She's very capable.'

'Capable of what? You surely don't expect me to let her set foot in this house, do you?'

'She won't do you any harm.'

'That's not the point. I am not in the habit of opening my house to riff-raff.'

'She's not riff-raff.'

'What is she then? There's no point in arguing, I shan't have her here and that's that.'

'In which case, I can't go.'

'Will you make up your mind? You gave me the impression this whole thing is a matter of life and death. If it is go, go now. If it isn't, stop wasting my time.'

'I'm not going to leave you on your own.'

'Are you suggesting that I'm helpless?'

'No, but it's not long since you were in hospital and . . .'

'Not long? It's nearly a year and if I've survived that, I'll survive anything. Now, off you go.'

The argument went on for about another hour, but I finally had my way. I brought in everything she might need, did all the cooking – so Avril would only have to heat it up – and, after she had arrived with her little sparrow, showed her round then set off for Dorset.

I wasn't sure what to expect.

Walter and his sister lived in a village which was hardly more than a street, in a white-washed cottage which must have been built just after the war, but, as I rang the bell again and again with no answer I was afraid I had made the journey for nothing. They could have been away for the day or on holiday. Since they had no 'phone I couldn't have told them I was coming, but I should have sent a telegram. Eventually a neighbour came to my help, who told me Walter was out with his sister.

'She's a bit funny, his sister, you see, and he never lets her out on her own,' and as we were talking they appeared over the brow of the hill, walking together hand in hand.

137

There was, at first sight, nothing funny about her. She was a grey-haired woman, well-dressed and well-kept, but her cheeks were sunken, her lips were chapped and shrivelled and she used a lot of spittle as she talked.

'You're Phyllis,' she said as soon as she saw me, 'thin, small and with glasses, just as Walter described you.' Walter stood beside her, grinning sheepishly, but not saying a word, and obviously pleased to see me. They had just got back from their weekend shopping in a nearby town.

She made a slap-up tea – scones, muffins and cakes – which she had baked all herself, but she didn't stop talking for a moment:

'You don't know how nice it is to see you. Walter told me a lot about you. He doesn't normally have much to say, Walter, but he told me how he'd met you in Frinton and thought he'd never see you again, and how you suddenly turned up one afternoon from nowhere, he couldn't believe you were there. Well that happens to me all the time. I keep thinking people are there, when they're not, or at least everybody else says they're not, and he thought it wasn't really you until he saw it was. He's probably not sure it's you now, but I know it is, because you're exactly as he said you were, thin, small and with glasses . . .' And so it went on. Walter didn't say a word, partly because he was busy enjoying the tea, cup after cup, first with muffins, then the scones, piling the butter on top of the jam, and jam on top of the butter, and then the cakes, and for that matter, I didn't get a chance to speak either.

I wanted to have a minute or two with him alone but I couldn't see how, especially as the last bus was due to leave in about an hour.

When I mentioned the bus she said: 'Oh, but you must stay for supper. I'm a very good cook, aren't I, Walter?'

'She's a very good cook,' said Walter.

'That's very kind of you, but you see I'm looking after an old lady . . .'

'Yes, he told me. Did you know that Walter once looked after an admiral, a full admiral, wasn't he Walter?'

'No, a Rear Admiral . . . was it at Jutland?'

138

'Yes, at Jutland. He has met some interesting people. I hardly meet anyone, real people, I mean, that's why I keep seeing unreal people I suppose . . .'

She talked while we were having tea, she talked as she was clearing up, she talked while she was washing up, and finally, in order to keep the noise of her shrill voice out of my head, I said I had to go out to make a 'phone call.

'I'll take you to the 'phone box,' she offered.

'No, no, I'm sure I can find it myself,' and I looked hard at Walter in the hope that he might offer to come with me, but he was busy helping his sister and didn't get the message.

It was a relief to be outside and have only the wind whistling in my ears. I didn't know what to do next. It seemed to me that if I intended to catch the bus I would have wasted a day. On the other hand if I stayed overnight I could be wasting two days, and I wasn't sure if the Old Woman could be left overnight. In any case, I had told her I was only going away for a day, and to take two days, even with her permission, was a liberty.

I decided to leave it to the Old Woman. If she agreed to my staying over and Avril would be able to stay with her, I'd stay over, but if she or Avril hummed or hawed, I'd go back.

But there was no problem either with her or Avril: 'Stay as long as you like,' they both told me, almost in the same words, and left me feeling a bit uneasy. They sounded as if they'd been drinking.

The sister prepared a simple but delicious supper, talking while she was cooking, serving, eating, clearing away and washing up, and I was afraid she would go on all night, but about nine she apologized that she was very tired, which didn't surprise me a bit, and went upstairs to bed, leaving Walter and me in front of the television. It was a black and white set – somebody had given it to them as a present, with a faulty picture – and since it always looked as if it was snowing it made me feel at home. I was in an easy chair on one side, and he on the other. It was a tiny room, lit by the glow of a gas fire. We weren't far apart, but he did not try to draw nearer.

'Your sister's a good cook,' I said.

'She is, isn't she?'

'I'm surprised she never married, good cooks are always in demand.'

'No, no, she's a bit old for that.'

'She's a bit what?'

'She's a bit old for that.'

'I didn't mean now.'

He turned the set down so that we could talk more easily.

'No, I don't know why she never married. Never fancied anyone, I suppose, or maybe nobody fancied her. She's a bit funny, you know.'

'She seems perfectly normal to me.'

'Yes, but she can turn funny. They only let her out on condition I stay with her. The funny thing is she's all right when I'm around – talks a lot, but then so did my wife – though there's no saying when she'll have another turn.'

'So you can't leave her by herself at all?'

'Oh yes, I can, and I do all the time. I'm out of the house at seven and I'm not back until four, but I wouldn't let her go to town on her own, or leave her overnight.'

'What would happen if you did?'

'Maybe nothing, but I think they'd want her back inside if I did. And she wasn't happy inside. Not that she complained. They wasn't nasty to her or anything like that, but she didn't eat and lost weight, and was covered with sores, and started wetting her bed. She wanted to come out, she said, but they wouldn't let her out, not on her own, so when I came to see her last Christmas I decided to stop here. I got a job with the local council looking after the grass verges and the cemetery and they let her out. Well, she's been a different woman since. I mean she talks a lot, but then so did my wife and I get used to that. You're about the only woman I've met what doesn't.'

'And I suppose you'll be stopping here for good to look after her.'

'Well we've got this council house here, you see, and I've got this job with the council, so there's no point in going anywhere else, is there? But I wouldn't say I look after her. It's more like she looks after me. She does the cooking, cleaning, mending and a bit of gardening besides. We grow all our spring vegetables. She's very good in the garden. Talks to the plants, I think they must like it, specially the brussel sprouts. You should see them, firm and round like golf balls. She talked to the chickens too, but I don't think they liked it so much because they've stopped laying you see. Might as well wring their necks and eat them, but she won't let me touch them.'

'Do you get worried when she talks to the chickens?'

'No, but I do when she thinks the chickens are talking to her. There was a time when she thought the vegetables was talking to her, and the flowers, and not only talking. She called me out one evening to listen to the geraniums. "Listen?" I said. "Listen," she said "very carefully. They're singing in chorus, such a lovely song", but that was some time back. It hasn't happened since I got back, and that's nearly a year. Of course it may be she talks so much herself that the flowers don't get a chance, but she's a different woman.

'But you still can't leave her?'

'Well I could, but there's no telling if she'd still be here if I got back.'

'So you're more or less here for good?'

'Yes, I suppose I am. Can't see how I'd be better off anywhere else. It would be nice to get away for a bit, but we can't because she doesn't like to leave the chickens, you see. The neighbours offered to look after them, but she doesn't know if the chickens would take to them.'

'So in fact you're happy here.'

'Oh yes, yes. Mind you, I was happy with the Admiral. Remember the old Admiral? He was at Jutland, you know. He needed a lot of looking after, but I liked keeping busy. And I was happy at the school if it comes to that. I'd never have left if it wasn't for her going funny like that.'

'So you miss your wife?'

'My wife?' He giggled. 'You know I've almost forgotten I was ever married. My sister doesn't like me to talk about it. Her and the wife never got on, you see. Not that the wife and I got on all that well either. I mean we didn't *not* get on, but we didn't get on either. She thought I was messy, that was the trouble. I took me boots off before I came into the house, but she complained I could make a mess even in me carpet slippers, and I think she'd rather I stopped in one place and didn't walk at all.'

The room was becoming so warm that I took off my cardigan. He was in a waistcoat and shirt sleeves. I gazed into the fire in silence.

'I'd better make up your bed,' he said. 'Will you be all right down here on the couch? I could let you have my bed upstairs, but we didn't know you was coming and we haven't changed the sheets.'

'No, I'll be fine here. You don't even have to make up a bed. I can stretch myself out on the couch.'

'But I have to be up early tomorrow, and I'll disturb you once I'm about.'

'That's fine. I have to be up early myself. I can't leave the Old Woman on her own for too long.'

'So you won't be stopping for lunch or anything like that?'

'I'm afraid not.'

'I'll be finished by lunch-time and I could show you the cemetery. It's a lovely cemetery. Beautiful lawns. The vicar said you could play croquet between the stones.'

'Maybe some other time.'

'My sister doesn't get up too early. She'll be upset if you leave before she's up. I'll wake her.'

'No, no, that won't be necessary, you can give her my apologies.'

'As a matter of fact you pass the cemetery in the bus.'

'I'll look out for it when I'm passing.'

'It's the drainage that makes the difference, you know. You can mow and roll, roll and mow for as long as you like, but if the place isn't drained properly you can do nothing with it.'

I don't know how long he went on about drainage and the cemetery for I must have fallen asleep, and when I woke a bed had been made up on the couch, and he was out of the room.

I undressed slowly, half hoping that he might barge in, but he didn't. I then sat up in bed hoping that he might come down. And again he didn't. I wondered why, if he had been so

142

keen to take his chances in Frinton, when there was every risk of getting caught wet-handed (which he nearly was), he didn't take his chance now, when there was no risk at all. It had been summer then and it was autumn now, but that shouldn't have made that much difference. Had something happened in between? It was more than two years ago, but I suppose when men get to a certain age two years can make all the difference. Or maybe it was simply that the thrill he was after was in the risk, and not in the other thing.

I didn't have much sleep that night and kept nodding off in the bus the next day. I had wasted two days, to say nothing of the fare, but I didn't think my journey had been wasted. I hated uncertainties. Ever since that summer in Frinton, Walter had hardly been out of my mind, and I kept thinking, especially late at night, what would have happened if he had stopped longer at the hotel or if we had had the opportunity to meet again, and to be alone, *really* alone, together. Now I had the answer – nothing. It meant that I no longer had anything to hope for or look forward to, or build fancies round, but it also meant that I knew where I was, and I liked to know where I was even if I had no great joy in being there.

I wasn't looking forward to seeing the Old Woman, because although she didn't ask me many questions, she was a shrewd old bird and must have known why I was so anxious to get away. And she was so ready to let me go because she must have guessed that I would come back empty-handed, and she would greet me when I got back with a little triumphant smirk on her great pan, as if to say: 'I told you so.'

But she didn't. It was about noon when I got back and an ashen-faced Avril came to the door.

'My God, am I glad you're here. I'm at my wits' end.'

She had brought the Old Woman a cup of tea at about nine in the morning, but she was asleep. She tried again an hour later and she was still asleep. When she hadn't stirred by eleven, she tried to wake her but couldn't. It was now after twelve and she still hadn't stirred.

'You haven't called the doctor?' I said.

'No, I was afraid to. You see I wanted to pop out for a bit

143

last night so I popped something in her drink to make sure she was asleep.'

'What did you pop in?'

'A pill I give to the little woman, it's harmless, at least to the little woman.'

'Only one?'

'Maybe two – she's a big woman. It might even have been three, I can't remember the exact number because I kept slipping them to her all evening. But look, I can't stop. I have to be back. We're expected for tea.' And in a few minutes she had bundled the sparrow into the car and was off.

I went upstairs and found the Old Woman sitting up in bed blinking her eyes and looking dazed and bewildered.

It took her a few seconds to get me into focus, then she said: 'Where's my cup of tea? And what are you doing with that coat on? It's not that cold in the house.' She seemed to have forgotten that I'd been away.

13

WINTER SEEMED TO come early that year and the weather was more than a talking point when you had to keep totting up the cost of the heating.

We stopped using the central heating because when the fuel tank emptied we couldn't afford to refill it. And since we couldn't use the electric heaters either, because the house needed rewiring, I got hold of a pair of second-hand paraffin heaters at a jumble sale and we used them instead. They weren't all that cheap, and they smoked a bit, but they had a nice cosy smell.

The smell might have been cosier if first Rigby, and then Digby (or maybe it was the other way about) hadn't become incontinent and started leaving their mark all over the place. I don't know how they did it, for they didn't seem to move about at all, but if I went out for a minute I would come back and find puddles under the curtains, near the fire-place, in the fire-place, by the beds, under the beds, by the stairs, on the stairs. I could almost imagine the one saying to the other: 'She's out, now's our chance, quick.'

'Poor, poor dears,' the Old Woman kept saying, 'how awful for them.' And I pointed out more than once that it was no joy for me either, and I said to her:

'Why don't you put them out of their misery?'

'I'll put you out of yours first.'

She was still quick in answering back, but slowing down in every other way, and she was even getting a bit soft.

Apart from regular events in the calendar like Christmas, and Crossleys, she could be sure, once the cold weather set in, to have a funeral or two to attend. When she was younger

145

they used to upset her, or at least I thought they did, but then, as she got on a funeral was about the nearest thing to good news. It meant somewhere to go to, people to see, old times to chat about, and she would come away with a slight look of triumph on her face, as if she had come through another round in some sort of elimination dance.

Then one day Lamb the butcher died. It had beeen a blow when she could no longer afford to buy his meat and an even bigger blow when the shop eventually closed, but old Lamb himself was something else. He was eighty-four and had been very ill for some time, and when he died everybody said it was a mercy. He had, in fact, outlived most of his customers, so there weren't all that many people at the funeral, and those who came were not usually the type the Old Woman mixed with, but she insisted on staying there. Sadly, though, for a day or two afterwards she could hardly eat, hardly speak, even to her dogs, and if I had had a suspicious turn of mind – which I don't – I might have thought that there had been more than one type of meat passing between old Lamb and her. Either that or she was getting soft, and then something happened which made me think that she was not only getting soft but had gone soft.

Emily still wrote to me every now and again. I wouldn't call her letters exciting because they were mostly about the weather (bad), or her sister's health (very bad). I didn't worry more about the one than about the other because, from what I saw of Bertha, I was perfectly sure that, ill as she was, she would outlive Emily. But she didn't, and one day I got a letter beginning: 'Dearest Phyllis, I don't know how to break it to you, but poor Bertha has passed away . . .' I felt like going out to celebrate, but the Old Woman was surprisingly sympathetic and suggested that I ask Emily to stay with us for Christmas. I thought I hadn't heard her right.

'Emily? Here? For Christmas?'

'Why not, the poor unfortunate. You can't leave her out there in the fens on her own, not at Christmas.' Emily was overcome with the invitation, as I knew she would be.

'Oh no, how can I? It would be presuming, and I'm still

146

having trouble with my legs, so I couldn't even make myself useful, and I'm not really sure if I can afford it, for travel is so dreadfully expensive. Poor Bertha wanted a simple funeral, but I couldn't make it too simple, and I'm afraid it rather put me out of pocket, but it is nice to be asked, and I really am very grateful . . .'

I half thought of sending her a postal order to pay for the train fare out of my own pocket, but knowing Emily she wouldn't have taken it and might even have been upset that I was treating her like a poor relative.

I wasn't looking forward to Christmas, not if it meant being alone with the Old Woman and her two dogs. It would have made a change to see a new face, even if it was only an old one like Emily's. I suppose that was why the Old Woman had thought of inviting her. Emily's memory was flickering on and off, but she remembered last Christmas as well as I did and was probably dreading a repeat. Last year I had lied that the vicar had asked us round for Christmas dinner. This year I had the feeling that if I told her the same she would have asked me to accept, so I specially went to church the first Sunday in Advent, just in case, but I got no invitation and he didn't even ask how the Old Woman was. She hadn't shown her face in church for a year.

In fact she hardly showed her face anywhere, mainly because of the dogs. They were too heavy and poorly to be taken out, and she didn't like to leave them on their own and I even had to do the Christmas shopping alone. There wasn't all that much to buy. She told me to get myself my traditional bottle of Guinness, 'something manly' for Coggeshall (a shoe horn), and 'something really nice, but not expensive ' for his clerk, Stanley (a pair of mock silver cuff-links), and, most surprisingly of all, 'something little, very little' for Emily (a bar of perfumed soap). I was surprised she could even think about Christmas presents because, from what I could see, she had more or less given up paying her bills.

It hadn't occurred to me how long people who had the status that goes with money can get by without paying bills; I suppose living in a large house (even if it was falling to pieces,

147

had something to do with it). The milkman called week after week, asking to be paid. When I couldn't face him any more, she came to the door, and told him that she had no money. He seemed satisfied with that, or at least, he still delivered the milk.

She didn't pay her paper bill either, but the *Mail* kept coming every day, and the *Radio Times* every week, and *Country Life* every month. The electricity, gas, water and rates remained unpaid, and as far as I could see no one tried to cut off anything. She still paid me regularly, more or less, but always grudgingly, but then she had always been grudging about it, even when she had had money.

One morning I noticed that one of the small panes in the front window was broken. It took me the better part of a day to find a glazier and when I told her what it would cost to mend the pane, she said:

'Not the whole window, silly, only one of the little panels.'

'I know,' I said, 'he was talking about one of the little panels.'

'But that's robbery,' which it was, so instead of having the pane repaired, I took out the bits of broken glass and blocked up the space with a small piece of cardboard.

It hadn't occurred to me that breakages are contagious, but they are because cracks soon developed in several of the other panes. Soon I had pieces of cardboard covering the whole window, and the old Woman complained that there was hardly any daylight coming into the house, and that we had to have the electric lights on all the time.

'It might be cheaper to get a glazier in now,' I said.

'No it won't.'

Then we had trouble with the plumber, the trouble being that there was no plumber about, or rather there wasn't for the sort of job we wanted. The kitchen tap was dripping so badly that the noise got on her nerves.

'Drop everything else. Forget about the cooking, the cleaning and the shopping. I want a plumber, that's all, a plumber.'

I eventually got one but it was the story of the glass panel all over again, so we just let the tap drip.

One dark morning I woke with the familiar stench of Rigby and Digby's doings in my nostrils and, as I did every morning, I got out a bucket, filled it with soap suds and disinfectant and set to work, first on one puddle, then on the next. I was working on a third one when I saw something which looked like a discarded teddy-bear at the bottom of the stairs. I went over to have a closer look and found Digby (or was it Rigby?) on his back, with his little stumpy legs in the air, his eyes open, his teeth bared, dead. I was so upset that I sat down on the stairs and almost cried. How would I break it to the Old Woman? How would she take it?

I then remembered Rigby (or was it Digby?) and began searching for him to see if he was all right, and found him asleep and snoring on the Old Woman's bed.

I put the poor little corpse in a cardboard box, put it out in the garden, and went back to my cleaning, when I heard the Old Woman calling me at the top of her voice.

'Phyllis, where are you Phyllis?' I rushed to her bed. 'Phyllis, where is Digby? He's always on my bed first thing in the morning, always. What's happened to him? Where has he gone?'

'Isn't that him on the bed?'

'That's Rigby, you fool. Can you find him?'

'I'll bring you a cup of tea.'

'No, no, damn your tea. I want Digby,' and she got out of her bed, but her legs gave way under her so I put her back inside.

'Leave it to me,' I said. 'I'll find him.'

I went to the kitchen wondering what to do next. There seemed nothing for it but to tell her straight out. At first she seemed perfectly calm.

'I knew it. I had the feeling that something had happened to him as soon as I woke. Bring him to me, poor little beast.'

I went to the garden, tidied him up a bit, and brought him in, and for the first time since I'd known her she broke down and cried. The tears poured down in torrents, soaking her nightie and her sheets.

'Poor, poor little beast,' she cried, hugging him close, 'how can I live without you?'

149

Rigby woke at the commotion and looked from her to me with bewilderment, and a few minutes later he keeled over and died too.

'It's a mercy,' she sobbed. 'He couldn't have lived on his own. They were two parts of one soul. If only I could die like him.' And for a time I thought she might.

She wouldn't stop crying but sat up in bed hugging the dead dogs to her bosom and swaying back and forward.

She wouldn't have anything to eat or drink and when she still refused food in the evening I picked up the 'phone to call Dr Boxer but the line was dead. I went out to the nearest call-box, called Boxer and then told the operator that our line was out of order. She checked the line, and said that it wasn't out of order, but had been cut off because we hadn't paid the bill.

Boxer gave her a sedative and told me to bury the dogs or have them cremated.

'She'll go off her head when she finds out,' I said.

'She's already gone off her head,' he said, 'and we may have to do something about that.'

I buried them that night, in the back garden. I felt a bit guilty like a criminal getting rid of his victim. And in a way I was guilty. I had wished them dead, and that's precisely what they were. I would have to be careful with my wishes.

She was much better the next morning and had a cup of tea when I brought it to her, but I was still dreading what she would say when I told her what I had done with the dogs. I could see her sending me back out into the garden to exhume them, but to my surprise she thought I had done the right thing. By chance the first of the Christmas cards had arrived that very morning. It was from a firm of monumental masons who had made the tombstone for her husband, and she talked about having a memorial stone carved for the dogs.

'I'll get a sculptor to do it, of Rigby and Digby in their prime. Remember how frisky they were, bless them? Fluff balls. And perhaps with a few lines of poetry underneath.' And she began composing a poem there and then: 'Rigby and Digby were brothers, Rigby and Digby were twins. Rigby and Digby entered my life . . .'

The next day we had a caller, a young woman with large glasses and short hair who said she was a 'Health Visitor.'

'A what?' I said.

'Health visitor. I'm from the local authority. Your doctor spoke to us yesterday. I understand you need help.'

I didn't need help and I took it she was talking about the Old Woman, who was still asleep. In the meantime I asked her in and made her a cup of tea.

'It's cold here,' she said, 'isn't it? Have you no heating at all?'

'Yes, a couple of paraffin stoves, but they take a bit of time to get going.'

'And is there any heating in the bedrooms?'

'There is downstairs, but not upstairs. We hardly use the upstairs rooms.'

She asked if she could see them, which seemed rather nosey of her, but she seemd a nice young woman and I didn't want to seem rude saying no, so I took her up. I hadn't been in what used to be the Old Woman's bedroom for some days, and I noticed that the wall-paper, which had been bulging in places, was beginning to come away from the wall.

'The place does need redoing, but she hasn't the money for it, or at least if she has, she doesn't want to spend it. I can't remember when we last had the painters in.'

The young woman stood there clutching the coat collar round her face as if she was in the eye of a storm, saying nothing. She looked as if she was trying to hold her breath.

'Can I see the old lady?' she asked.

'Not if she's asleep. I don't like to wake her.'

'Shall I come back in the afternoon then?'

'No, she rests in the afternoon. The best time to catch her's in the evening, but early in the evening, because we go to bed early – it's the cheapest way of keeping warm.'

We went downstairs and she almost ran out of the house.

When the Old Woman woke up I told her about our visitor.

'A health visitor?' she said. 'Probably some busybody from the Town Hall. I hope you didn't let her in.'

'You were asleep, so I asked her in for a cup of tea.'

151

'You had no right to. You're beginning to take liberties, treating the house as if it's your own. Did you give her the Earl Grey?'

'Earl Grey? We haven't been buying Earl Grey since the summer.'

'Even ordinary tea costs money, and even if it doesn't I don't like busy-bodies from the Town Hall sniffing about the house. Can't even have five minutes rest without you opening the house to busy-bodies.'

'Boxer sent for her.'

'Boxer? He had no right to. If he's going to start poking his nose into my business I'll get another doctor. You'd think he had enough to keep him busy without poking his nose into other people's business. What did she want?'

'The health visitor?'

'The health visitor.'

'She thought we needed help.'

'She thought we needed what?'

'Help.'

'What sort of help? Could she mend the windows or stop that infernal tap from dripping? Can she mend the 'phone?'

'The 'phone isn't broken. They've cut us off because you haven't paid the bills.'

'I've been paying bills all my life and I've had enough of it. Did you tell her that?'

'She had nothing to do with the 'phone.'

'And I don't suppose she had anything to do with the taps or the windows either.'

'She didn't.'

'Then what do you mean she thought we needed help, when from what you tell me she seemed perfectly helpless herself. In future, if we're not expecting callers, don't open the door. Can't even rest for five minutes without you opening the door to busy-bodies.'

Two Christmas cards arrived, which cheered her up a bit, one from Emily, and another from a laundry which we hadn't used since the summer. I got out her cord and fixed it along the mantelpiece and put the cards over it.

'What date is it?' she asked.

'Tenth of December.'

'We have two weeks to go, at this rate we could have a full cord.'

The next day she received a fourth card – from the lady with the electric chair she had met at Frinton – and when I saw how it cheered her up I had a word with a road-crossing attendant who sometimes chatted with us as we waited to cross the road, and he also sent her a card. Another from the Queen Anne Hotel in Frinton brought the number up to six, from Coggeshall to seven and I went out and bought an eighth. She expected a ninth from Crossleys but it didn't come which spoilt things a bit.

We didn't buy a turkey that year, but a small chicken which I stuffed with stale bread and other odds and ends, so that it bulged like a turkey. The back garden was like a jungle with all sorts of things growing in it, so that I wasn't short of holly or anything like that, and I brought in so much greenery of different sorts that the Old Woman complained that I was making the place look like Kew Gardens. But I still wasn't looking forward to spending Christmas alone with her, and prayed for a last minute reprieve, an unexpected guest or, better still, an unexpected invitation. And so, I suppose, did she. And would you believe it, our prayers were answered.

I was in the Old Woman's room one evening, watching television, when everything suddenly went black and the only light in the room was a pale glimmer from the paraffin stove. At first I thought it was a fuse, which I had learned to mend myself, but it wasn't and as our 'phone was still cut off, I went out to the call-box to call an electrician, but the call-box was also out of order so I knocked on the door of the nearest house, which was an architect's or designer's office of some sort, and asked if I could use their 'phone. It was still early in the evening, but I couldn't get hold of an electrician, and a man called Harvey, who was working at a drawing board, kindly asked if he could be of help. He brought a torch, and spent about an hour over the lights but couldn't get them back on. He came again the next morning with a man called Eric, and after rummaging around for a bit in the cellar they managed to repair the fault. The wires had apparently been bitten through by rats. 'Don't tell the Old Woman,' I said, 'she'll have hysterics.'

I wasn't really sure that she would, but I nearly did. I couldn't believe it.

'Are you sure it was rats? I haven't seen one.'

'You wouldn't up here, but try and look in the cellar. If I was you I would call the pest people in the town hall.'

Well a friendship of sorts grew out of that visit and the next day Harvey invited the Old Woman and me to Christmas dinner.

14

THE INVITATION BROUGHT colour back into the Old Woman's cheeks, and a whole evening passed without her mentioning her dogs once.

'He was so beautifully spoken, that I knew he was a gentleman. What is his wife like? I must get her something nice for Christmas.'

I couldn't even remember seeing his wife, and as she spoke, something else occured to me. I had forgotten to ask where he lived. I went round to his office the next morning and asked for his home address, and he looked at me non-plussed.

'We live here, on the next floor.'

The Old Woman had been a bit worried about the cost of getting there – he could live miles out – but when I told her that it was his home as well as his office, and just two hundred yards down the road, she cursed herself for not having invited him in before.

'I thought we were the last private household in the neighbourhood.'

'We were. I think they only moved in a few weeks ago.'

She sent me out to buy a pot plant as a present, and I helped to do her hair, and to get her into her black velvet dress with the lace collar which took a bit of doing, for she seemed to grow larger with every passing Christmas. When she finally got it on I was afraid it might come apart during the meal. Then she took it off and tried the brown dress with the beaded bodice, but as I forced up the zip the beads began to fly in all directions, like bird-shot, so it was back to the black dress. I don't know if she was happier with it, but I was. Christmas wouldn't have seemed Christmas without it.

She then began searching around for her jewels and seemed to have quite forgotten that my dear brother Arthur had taken them all, together with the other valuables in the house, and I was afraid to remind her in case it set off another attack.

'Could I have put them in the safety deposit box at the bank?' she asked.

'You could have done,' I said, which wasn't quite a lie, and I added. 'You look just right in that dress. You'd be overdoing it a bit if you had jewellery.'

'I would not. My diamond earrings were bought to go with this dress. You should have reminded me to get them out for Christmas. You always leave me to think of everything.'

Since it was a mild evening she insisted on going on foot. She took both her sticks, but even so I had to half carry her there.

Eric came to the door and she nearly toppled backwards at the sight of him, for he wore a ruffled shirt, bangles and a pair of golden earrings. He was also heavily perfumed. I didn't recognize him in that outfit and with that smell, and at first thought we had come to the wrong door, but he greeted us with a loud: 'How nice to see you,' and kissed the Old Woman on her hand.

'Our flat's on the top floor, do you think you'll be able to make it? They're quite steep. Not very thoughtful of us, we could have arranged the meal in the drawing office downstairs.'

'No, no, I can make it,' she insisted.

And make it she did, though she nearly fell back on top of us a dozen times for she kept catching her feet and her sticks in the folds of her dress.

Harvey met us at the top in a striped apron.

'Do forgive my appearance,' he said, 'I'm just putting the finishing touches to the meal and it's all taking a little longer than I'd anticipated.' He had no earrings or bangles, and smelled of garlic and wine.

We went through a narrow passage lined with framed prints and into a large room. There was an open fire and a polished round table, set for the meal with gleaming cutlery, crystal wine glasses and linen napkins.

Afterwards, the Old Woman said I'd made a pig of myself,

which I suppose I had, but I wasn't used to the sort of hospitality we received. Usually at Christmas she gave me a tiny wine glass, and when I emptied it, it stayed empty. This time I was given a large glass, and when I emptied it they refilled it so that long before we were on the main course I was in a merry haze. I only realized how much I had had when I got up to help clear the table and felt as if I was walking on water. I came away with only a vague idea of what I had said or done, but, according to the Old Woman, I'd kept putting my hand on Eric's knee and complimenting him on his looks. I had also asked him if he was married, and when he said 'no,' I asked him why not, and I also asked to try on his earrings.

'But that was the least of it,' she said, 'it was the things you told him about yourself which made my hair curl.'

'Why? What did I tell him?'

'What didn't you tell him? Who was Walter?'

'Walter.'

'Eric was rash enough to ask if there were any men in your life, and you were rash enough to tell him, at great length, and in indelicate detail, accompanied by shrieks of coarse laughter, all coming from your self. I can assure you no one else was amused, and at least one person was painfully embarrassed.'

'Why? What did I say?'

'I am too much of a lady to repeat it.'

I would never have believed that one meal could change the whole life of a person. Ever since we returned to Frinton she had complained that everything was going to pieces, everyone was dying, and so was she, which was a mercy, because she could no longer afford to live. When the dogs died I wasn't sure if she would live through Christmas or if I would either, but now, for the first time she began to look forward to things, to the new year, to Crossleys, even to the summer. Harvey and Eric left for a skiing holiday immediately after Christmas, but she planned to have them round to dinner and spoke about preparing the meal herself. She seemed a new woman. It reminded me of the remissions poor mother had during her last illness. I would sometimes come into her room and find her sitting up with life in her eyes, and even a bit of colour in her cheeks, and for a day or two she would talk not like an invalid, but a woman who happened to be in bed for a rest, but it wouldn't last, and neither did this. I suppose the sudden change in weather had something to do with it. Christmas had been bright and nippy with clear blue skies, but then the sun went in and stayed in, everything turned grey for days on end and a shrill wind blew, cold, moist and gritty, which cut to the very marrow, and even in the mornings shopping was an ordeal. The Old Woman couldn't get out of the house, and didn't even get out of bed. Then the light kept flickering off, and finally stayed off but, as Harvey and Eric weren't around to repair it, she refused even to talk about getting an electrician; we were left in twilight and darkness. I suppose the rats had been at the wires again so I 'phoned the town hall to ask if they were going to do anything about it.

And then came a really cruel blow. As a rule the first post after Christmas was the invitation to the Crossley preview. And the usual card arrived in the usual large white envelope, with Crossleys written in the corner. She opened it and put the card on her mantelpiece without even bothering to read it, or rather, as she didn't have her glasses on, she couldn't read it, but she didn't have to because the preview was always on the second Saturday in January. It gave a lift-off to the year, but it was me who noticed that it wasn't an invitation to the preview, but to a closing-down sale. I couldn't quite believe it, and I blurted out: 'Crossleys closing down?'

'What was that?'

'It says that Crossleys are closing – but they couldn't be.' I brought her glasses. They were. She read and reread the announcement in a trembling voice. I was upset, so I could imagine how she felt. She complained often enough that she missed the sight of the Crossley van coming up the street, and the Crossley man, in his green livery, coming to the door, but even if she could no longer make her monthly order, as long as Crossleys was in business she felt her world was in order and that England was still England.

'I got my trousseau in Crossleys, they furnished this house, the crockery is Crossleys, the cutlery. Do you remember the teas we used to have there on Wednesday afternoons, and the lunches?'

The lunches and teas must have been before my time, but I didn't interrupt her.

'Their corsetière was the best in England. Her mother used to look after my mother, and she looked after me. I was thinking of going to see her after Christmas. Can't think where else I can go.' She looked at the card again, to see if it was really true, and sighed like a burst tyre.

She didn't say anything more, she didn't have to. Her face said everything, there was nothing left to live for.

Nothing could console her after that, not even the news that her sister had died. If anything it made things worse. Her sister was an unmentionable, but as long as she was alive I think the Old Woman felt she had to keep on going, if only to outlive her. Now that she was dead, she could relax and die quietly herself.

We went through a fortune in candles in those few days, for even if we went to bed early at night, it wasn't all that light during the day and we had candles going all the time. But that wasn't the worst of it. Once we stopped using the central heating, our water, which was heated by electricity, also stopped. I somehow managed with household chores by boiling kettle after kettle on the gas, and I didn't mind washing myself in cold water, but the Old Woman did and she began to smell worse than her dogs. I couldn't tell her that of course, or at least I could, but she was a bit sorry for herself as it was, and I didn't want to add to her miseries. Instead, I made what I thought were subtle hints, such as: 'Have you ever washed in cold water? It's a lovely way of starting the day, makes you feel nice and fresh.'

'Cold water? When I was at school we never washed in anything else. I had chilblains from November till March.'

'Well if you prefer hot water I could put a kettle on.'

'A kettle? What good will that do?'

'I could give you a going over with a sponge.'

'I'll give you a going over with the kettle.'

The worst thing was that as the Old Woman was hardly out of bed, I couldn't get in to clean her room, or at least to clean it properly. At first she had breakfast in bed, then it was lunch in bed and, finally, it was everything in bed. I tried to make non-spillable meals, but there is no way of making non-spillable tea or soup. Her sheets and pillows were greased and stained, but she wouldn't get out of bed long enough even to let me change her linen. Her bed, she said, was the only warm place in the house, and she would get out when the warmer weather came.

'It mightn't come till June.'

'I'm in no hurry.'

It was true that the paraffin stoves didn't give out much heat, especially in the really cold weather, and there were days when I went about my work in an overcoat, muffler and mittens.

One morning I went out to do the shopping and found the streets quiet and everything closed. As we had no electricity, we had no television and radio, and the papers for some reason – maybe because we had stopped paying for them – had stopped coming and it occurred to me that it could be Sunday. There was a man standing by a bus stop and I asked him what day it was, a perfectly polite question, I thought. He looked at me for a moment with something like alarm, and walked off, and when he saw I was going in the same direction he began to run. I eventually found a small Pakistani shop which was still open and managed to pick up a few things for supper.

When I had the meal ready she wanted me to keep her company in her room. I had to hold my breath when I was near her, and couldn't see myself holding down my food.

'No,' I said, 'it's unhygienic to eat in the bedroom. Come and have it in the kitchen.'

'It's too cold in the kitchen.'

'I'll bring the heaters in.'

'They're not much use either of them – give off more smoke than heat,' and finally she ate in her bedroom and I in the kitchen.

Something must have got into her, for she complimented me on the meal. Usually she complained. The previous day she'd accused me of making rissoles out of cat's meat, which is exactly what I'd done this time; not out of pique, it was the only thing I could afford with the money she gave me.

The next morning it was raining heavily, but it wasn't so cold, so I decided that even if I couldn't persuade her to have a wash, I would give her room a good going over if it was the last thing I did. As soon as she was up – the morning was half gone by then – I told her I was moving her out of the bed and into the living room.

'I'll freeze,' she screamed.

I was a bit startled by her voice. She didn't sound herself. I was always ready to argue with the Old Woman I knew, but this was an old woman I didn't know, but even if grass grew on her I couldn't leave the room in the state it was.

'Look,' I said, 'it's not so cold and I've had the heater on for hours. Apart from anything I've got to change your sheets.'

'You changed them yesterday.'

'I changed them last week and you've been eating in bed, drinking in bed, and I daren't think what else you've been doing in bed, and if you're not going to move yourself I'll have to turf you out.'

Her nightdress was torn and she sat up and folded her arms over her great floppy breasts with brambly hairs round the nipples and the key to the drinks cupboard dangling between them like a pectoral cross.

'Go on, try it,' she said. I don't know if I imagined it, but she seemed to have doubled her size in the past week. Her face was grubby, her hair was matted and bedraggled. She was never the lady she thought she was, but there had always been a slight touch of the gentry about her, not only in her manner and accent and voice, but in her looks. It all seemed to have gone in a matter of days. I kept looking at the great, sluttish drab and wondering who it was.

I grabbed her blankets, and she grabbed them back, and for a minute of so we had a tug-of-war, but I was no match for her bulk and it took me some time to get back my breath. I then tried again, but this time our game was interrupted by a ring at the door.

It was the young health visitor accompanied by a middle-aged man in a mock suede jacket with mock fur collar, and she introduced him as her superior.

They wanted to see the Old Woman. The Old Woman was not in a fit state to be seen, neither, for that matter, was her room, but I always had a respect for authority and I thought I had better tell her they were here. When I tried her door, however, it was locked.

'You've got visitors,' I said.

'Visitors? What visitors? I'm not expecting visitors.'

'Boxer asked them to come.'

'He had no business to do any such thing. I don't want to see anyone. Tell them to go. This minute. Now. I'll have something to say to Boxer when I see him, nasty little man.'

'Is she all right in there on her own?' asked the woman.

'Yes, why?'

'She's not suicidal?'

'Her? Homicidal, maybe, but not suicidal.'

They asked me if she had next-of-kin. As far as I knew there was no one, but I told them about Coggeshall and they took his address and telephone number and left.

She kept the door locked for the rest of the day and had me worried when I knocked and she didn't answer, but towards the evening she got hungry and opened the door to let me bring in her supper.

'Warmed up leftovers,' she grumbled.

'What do you expect?'

'A proper meal.'

'Proper meals cost proper money.'

'I bet you're having a proper meal, that's why you don't want to eat with me, you don't want me to see what you're having.'

Her voice sounded slurred. I wondered if she'd been at the drinks cupboard.

That night I was just settling down to sleep when I was awakened by voices coming from her room. At first I thought that I was imagining it, but I went downstairs and there she was sitting up in the darkness talking to herself. I stood over her, listening, and she rambled on, without noticing I was there.

'. . . no, no, the satin's too bulky, it makes me look fat. Now this is much softer and it fits snugly round the hips . . . Mildred, will you wait? Please wait Mildred, I won't be long. Mildred . . .' Then her words lost all meaning. She didn't seem to be speaking in English. I couldn't stay long because the room was icy and I was shivering. Also I found the smell a bit much. I opened the window a little to let some air in and went upstairs to bed. Later in the night I suddenly remembered that she was on the ground floor and someone could get in through the window. There wasn't anything left worth stealing, not after brother Arthur had had his pick, but I didn't like the thought of intruders, but as I went back downstairs to close the window, something dark scurried across my path and nearly frightened the life out of me. It was a rat.

The next morning when I brought her a cup of tea she said:

'Where's Rigby and Digby?'

'Where's who?'

'The dogs, Rigby and Digby. I like to have them on my bed.'

'It's not hygienic to have them on your bed.'

'What do you mean it's not hygienic?'

'They smell.'

'So do you. All living things have their own natural odour. They're entitled to smell. Where are they? I want them here this minute.'

'They're outside.'

'In this weather?'

'It's not cold.'

'It's wet, they could catch cold. I want them in here.'

'Now?'

'This minute.'

'They'll be wet.'

'I know they'll be wet you stupid woman, that's why I want them in here.'

I went out into the garden and walked around in a circle, wondering what to do next. I half thought of taking a can of paraffin, sprinkling it round the floor and setting fire to the whole building. It seemed so ugly and decrepit from the back, tiles falling off the roof, gutters broken or blocked, windows cracked, brickwork crumbling, paintwork peeling, woodwork warped. It was in about the same state as the Old Woman herself, but then I noticed broken branches and twigs

163

all over the place, and I began gathering winter fuel, like the poor man in Good King Wenceslas. I would make an open fire! I wondered why I hadn't thought of it before.

When I came into her room laden under the branches and twigs I must have looked like a walking wood for she got a fright.

'What on earth do you think you're doing?'

'I'm going to make a fire.'

'What about the dogs?'

'It's too cold here for the dogs, I'll make the fire first.'

'I have a horrible feeling that you've done something nasty to them.'

'To whom?'

'The dogs.'

'I haven't, but if you go on like that I'll do something nasty to you.'

When the fire was finally going, however, she stopped grumbling and even got out of bed, put on her dressing-gown and sat down in a chair by the hearth. She seemed to have forgotten about the dogs.

The branches and the twigs burned brightly and quickly. There was a line of trees at the bottom of the garden forming a sort of wall between us and our neighbours, and I took out an axe, loped off the branches I could reach, chopped them up into firewood and put them in the fire.

The fire not only warmed and brightened the room, it seemed to put new life into the Old Woman, but she didn't stop talking.

'We would have an open fire in the nursery, every day, from about the time we returned from holidays in September till after Easter. There was a metal guard in front of the fire on which nanny would dry our mittens, or she would remove it to make toast. And she would tell us stories, what marvellous stories. Mildred – little miss bossy-boots – would always spoil them by saying, "but it can't be true," that was her refrain in life, "it can't be true," and she called herself a Christian. The coals would crackle, and send out little jets and hisses, and the room would glow, and I could see all sorts of figures dancing in the flames. I can see them now . . .' Her voice gradually died away and she dropped off to sleep.

I quickly jumped to my feet and put a couple of kettles on. This was my chance. I would clean her room. I went upstairs to the linen cupboard and brought out some sheets and pillow cases. They were slightly damp, I put them down by the fire to dry, and pulled the sheets off her bed. At that moment the doorbell went.

To my surprise it was Coggeshall. As he entered he looked round with alarm.

'Is the place on fire?

I hadn't noticed it, but it was years since the chimney had been cleaned and the house was full of smoke. When he came into the bedroom he recoiled. The Old Woman was sitting with her head back, her mouth open her breasts out, bed- clothes were scattered all around the floor, and the place stank to heaven. He tried to switch the lights on, but of course they didn't work.

'What's happened to the lights?'

'The wiring's gone.'

'Gone? Why didn't you tell me? How long have you been without light? Has the heating gone as well? Where's the smell coming from?'

He went on like this for some minutes piling question on question without giving me a chance to answer. I lit a candle, but that didn't satisfy him and he went to his car and came back with a huge torch which he shone into the Old Woman's face. She didn't stir in spite of the light. She didn't look at all well. He asked me who was her doctor and his 'phone number. I told him, but added that he couldn't 'phone from here because the 'phone was cut off.

'The 'phone as well! Does nothing in this blessed house work? You were meant to be looking after her, is that how you do your duty?'

'I was looking after her, but it's not my fault if she didn't pay her bills.'

'Her bills? What bills?'

'All of them. You name them, she didn't pay them.'

'How long has this been going on for?'

'Since the summer.'

'Why didn't you 'phone me?'

'The 'phone's cut off, isn't it?'

'You could have written,' he shouted. 'Now go next door, ask if you can use their 'phone. Tell them it's urgent.'

'Who do you want me to 'phone?'

'The doctor, you fool, and be quick about it.'

I went and 'phoned. When I came back he was standing in the middle of the living room with a handkerchief to his face.

'What a mess! This place isn't fit for human habitation. Have you seen the upstairs rooms? Moisture and mildew everywhere, fungi climbing up the walls, its like a bloody mushroom farm, the paper peeling, the windows broken, no light, no heating, no 'phone and the poor old half-demented woman, half naked in a filthy night-gown. Is that how you look after her? Do you realize it's a criminal offence to leave a helpless old woman in such a state? You might have at least changed her sheets. Look at them.'

'What the hell do you think I was trying to do when you came in?'

'They should have been done weeks ago, before they got into this filthy state.'

'And how do you think they got into that state? Because I couldn't get her to shift her great, fat carcase out of her bloody bed.'

'You could have helped her. She was probably too poorly to move herself.'

'Helped her? I would have had to plant a stick of dynamite under her.'

'Do you mind not raising your voice to me?'

'You raised yours first.'

'I have every right to raise my voice. Never in my whole life have I come upon such a case of scandalous neglect.'

'You haven't, haven't you. Who's been neglecting whom then? You were her a few weeks ago, weren't you?'

'I was not, I was here some months ago.'

'Then you should have made it your business to have come down more often. I'm only her companion, you're supposed to be her solicitor. And if it comes to that things weren't all that

166

rosy when you were here, were they? You saw what the situation was then. Why didn't you do anything about it?'

'She was in robust health, when I was here last, well-dressed, well-kept, and very much in possession of her faculties.'

'She was, was she? Didn't you tell her she was out of her mind?'

'I was speaking metaphorically. You were here on the spot and could see what was happening. Good God, look around you. If you had kept pigs in this condition you'd have been summoned by the animal welfare people.'

'But pigs at least can move on their own steam and if they don't you can give them a kick to get them moving. You couldn't do that to her. Perhaps I should have done.'

'Now that's quite enough of that. Your impudence has passed all tolerable limits. It wouldn't be so bad if you were otherwise reliable, but you're not. You can't stop here another minute. You'll have to go.'

'I'll have to what?'

'I'll pay you four weeks' wages in lieu of notice, but you can't stay here, not another minute.'

I drew breath to tell him where to get off, but even as I was doing it I thought I'd call his bluff.

'All right,' I said, 'If that's how you feel about it, I'll go.'

But he wasn't bluffing. He took a large wallet out of his breast pocket and asked me how much I was getting, which took the wind right out of my sails.

'How much?'

'How much what?'

'Your wages. How much did she pay you?' It was too late to pull back now, and in a voice which sounded oddly meek to my ears I told him.

'But you were getting that two or three years ago.'

'Was I?'

I wasn't sure if he meant that she was paying me too much or too little, but in the end he paid me more than four weeks' wages, a hundred pounds in fact, in twenty-pound notes. I had never handled so much money in my life and it made me feel light-headed.

167

I went upstairs to pack. It seemed an unreal thing to do in the middle of winter. Packing was something we did in June for Frinton. If it wasn't for the cold and the frost I'd have thought I was going on holiday. I put on my coat and my hat. Hats were something I never wore but I had this hat which had belonged to my sister, it didn't fit into the case so the only thing I could do was to put it on my head. It was a large thing with a blue band and a floppy brim. I must have looked as if I was going to a garden party.

When I went downstairs Coggeshall was gone but his car was still in the drive. He had presumably gone out to make a phone call. The Old Woman was still asleep, her mouth open. I couldn't see how I could leave without saying good-bye, on the other hand I didn't want to wake her. But I couldn't believe I was leaving in the first place. Besides, how could I leave with the room in such a state? I took off my hat and coat, rolled up my sleeves and got on with what I'd been doing before Coggeshall turned up, and once I was busy I couldn't believe he had turned up and had told me to go. But then I looked up and there was this large car in the drive, and my suitcase all packed by the door, and my hat and coat slung over a chair. It was the hat more than anything else which brought the message home; I'd never have got it out of the cupboard unless I was going, and going for good.

I washed my hands, rolled down my sleeves, put on my hat and coat and was leaning forward to grasp the Old Woman's hand, when she opened her eyes and looked at me with a start. I suppose she didn't recognize me in that hat. Then she said:

'What are you doing? Where are you going? Why are you wearing that ridiculous hat?'

'I'm leaving.'

'You're what?'

'I'm leaving.'

'Leaving? What do you mean you're leaving? Who said you could leave?'

'Coggeshall . . .' but she didn't let me finish.

'Coggeshall? What's he got to do with it?'

'He was here a minute ago and told me to leave.'

168

'Coggeshall? What was he doing here? Who asked him to come? I won't have him in this house. Where is he?' She tried to rise to her feet but sank down and again I helped her into bed and made her comfortable. She was trembling with fury or cold (for the fire was dying out), maybe both.

'Just because he was in charge of the family trust – what's left of it – doesn't mean to say he can run my life. I wonder what gets into the man. How dare he tell you to leave? And in any case how could you think of leaving after all I've done for you? If I can't drop off for five minutes without having you walk out then perhaps I should better get someone more reliable. Is lunch ready? Or am I expected to starve as well as freeze?'

'I'll get it ready.'

'Wait. Before you do, take off that hat. It offends me.'

I had been in the kitchen for about five minutes when I heard voices – or rather a voice – coming from the bedroom. Coggeshall was back and she was giving him an earful, in tones which could have been heard two streets away, but I opened the door slightly to make sure I was missing nothing:

'What do you mean *you* told her? What *right* had you to tell her? Who do you think you are? You're only my solicitor, you know, not my butler, who are you to order people about?' Her voice was a high screech, his a low rumble, and he could hardly get a word out.

'She was what? Was she indeed? That's for me to say. I don't tell you how to run your practise, don't you tell me how to run my household. I know you think I'm senile. Yes, you do. You do, you think I'm senile but even if I am I've still got more wits about me than you've ever had in your prime. If you should *dare* . . .'

And then suddenly there was silence. I waited for more, but it didn't come. I put my head into the hall just in time to see Coggeshall throw the front door open and run down the drive as if the furies were after him. I had never seen anything of that size move so fast. Had she taken a knife to him, a gun perhaps? I had a couple of saucepans on the stove. I turned the gas down, took off my apron and went into the bedroom.

'Have you seen . . .' I began, and broke off. The curtains

169

were partly drawn, the fire had died out and the room was almost in darkness. She was sitting up in bed stiffly, her eyes wide open, her hands downwards on the quilt, as if she was trying to raise herself.

'Are you all right?' I said.

She didn't answer.

'I've got soup on the stove, it'll be ready in a jiffy. A bowl of soup is just what you need,' and I went back to the kitchen. You had to be sensible about these things. She was living or dead. If she was dead there was nothing I could do about it; if she was living she'd want a bowl of soup. But I couldn't believe she was dead, not the Old Woman. It wasn't like her. And besides people who can shout as she'd done only a minute before don't pop off just like that. And *I* could do with a bowl of soup even if she couldn't.

And so I made the soup, poured it into a bowl and went back to the bedroom. She was still there sitting upright, as I'd left her, as if she'd turned to stone. At that moment Boxer, Coggeshall and two ambulance men with a stretcher came rushing in.

'Too late I suppose?' said Coggeshall between puffs.

'Afraid so,' said Boxer.

He didn't take her pulse. How could he tell? I stood there with the bowl of soup in my hands saying nothing and feeling rather silly.

'I don't think she'll be wanting that,' said Boxer, 'but you look as if you could do with it.'

15

IT WAS A small funeral, the smallest I'd been to. There was only the vicar there, and me, old Stanley and a couple of old codgers I hadn't seen before, who looked as if they'd come along because they had nothing better to do. That was all. Even Fat Lord High and Mighty Coggeshall wasn't there. It was just as well the Old Woman was dead, for she'd have been upset at the small turn-out.

It was cold and foggy and the vicar's words came in bursts of steam as if he was angry with the Old Woman about something. I couldn't make out what he was saying, I suppose because I wasn't listening.

I suppose I should have been upset, but I wasn't, not a bit. In an odd way, as the coffin was lowered into the ground, and they began shovelling the yellow, moist clay, thump, thump, thump, on top of it. I even felt a little envious. There was something comforting about burials. I had been with her to a cremation once when she had said: 'My God, that was awful, it makes one want to hang on to dear life.' There's something terribly final about cremations, but not burials. It's not that I thought she'd rise again once the weather was better, but I did have the feeling that that wasn't quite the end.

When the ambulance men took her away, Coggeshall and the doctor went with them and left me alone in the empty house.

Cold though it was, I pulled open all the curtains, threw open all the windows and began a thorough spring cleaning job. I didn't have to think too much while I was busy, and I didn't want to think at that particular moment. There was a lot to do and I only managed to finish the downstairs rooms before it was too dark to continue.

I began again at first light the next morning and was just about finished when there was a knock on the door. It was old Stanley.

Though I had seen them take her away and I had folded her sheets and blankets and put away her wheelchair and her walking sticks, I still couldn't believe she was dead, until Stanley came to the door. He was a sort of local representative of the angel of death, and seeing him there with his bowler in hand made it official. He had come to lock up and take me to the funeral.

'What about the dirty linen?' I said. 'I haven't had a chance to wash it.'

'Mr Coggeshall said to leave everything and lock up.'

'It'll rot in the laundry basket.'

'You seem to be more worried about her dirty linen than you are about yourself. What are you going to do with yourself?'

I hadn't given it a thought. My main worry at the moment was what to do with my case – I could hardly take it to the funeral grounds, and Stanley had received strict instructions to lock everything up *before* the funeral.

In the end I put it in the boot of the car, not the hearse, but the car behind.

'Hadn't it occurred to you that she could be moving on,' Stanley asked, 'I mean, she was entitled to at her age.'

'I'm entitled to at my age, if it comes to that. My mother wasn't much older than me when she moved on, and my sister was no age at all.'

'Imagine talking like that. You're a young woman, at least you are compared to her, only you've got to learn to look after yourself.'

After the funeral he left me with my case in the centre of town and told me to 'phone him if there was anything I needed.

'I will,' I thought to myself, 'when I'm ready for burial.'

The fog had cleared and the air was sharp and fresh and it was a pleasure to breathe, but I felt odd, as if I'd just left prison after a long spell inside. I had no idea where to go or

172

what to do next. A passing policeman looked at me, and looked at my case, wondering, I supposed, if I'd nicked it. The more he looked at me, the more I began to feel that I *had* nicked it, and I moved on.

I had a hundred pounds in my bag and more than that in my post office savings account. I could treat myself to a foreign holiday if I wanted, but I didn't particularly want it. I suppose the rich went through that sort of thing all the time.

What with one thing and another I had forgotten to eat so I went to an Indian restaurant and had a plate of curry and a bottle of Guinness. I was the only one in the restaurant and the dark-skinned waiter waited impatiently for me to finish, but I spent more time in thinking than eating, but when I came out I still didn't know what to do.

I walked uphill to the park – the first time I had gone up that hill without pushing a chair in front of me – and it didn't seem nearly as steep as I thought, even though I was still carrying my case. It was very cold and the park was almost empty. I opened my case, took off my coat, and put on a warm jersey underneath. It somehow always seemed to be colder in the park than elsewhere in Crumpshall. I suppose because it was higher up and more open. I walked over to my favourite spot, which was the duck pond, and I sat there all alone with the ducks. They waddled towards me waiting for bread, but I had none to give them. I suppose if it had been warmer I would have jumped in, not out of despair or anything like that, but because I couldn't think of anything else to do, but it was very cold and the water was frozen over. Besides I had all that money in my handbag. It would be a terrible waste.

The sun began to set. The sky turned red and the ice looked as if it was on fire. I could hear a bell ringing in the distance. The park was closing. There wouldn't have been time for me to drown myself even if I'd wanted to.

I suppose it was watching the ducks which made me think of Emily, for she waddled like a duck.

I 'phoned her to ask if I could come and stay, and she was overjoyed to hear me.

'How marvellous! Would you believe it, but I was actually

173

praying for you to come. Is it going to be a long stay or a short stay?'

'Whatever you like.'

'I'd like you to stay for good.'

'It might come to that.'

'Might it? Are you serious? You're not making fun of me?'

'No, I'm not making fun of you.'

'What about the Old Lady? She can come as well if she likes. I could make up a room for her on the ground floor.'

'You can forget about the old lady.'

'You haven't quarrelled have you?'

'I'll tell you all about her when I see you.'

'But she is all right, isn't she?'

'She's as well as can be expected.'

'I *am* glad. Oh, we *shall* have fun.'

I put down the telephone and turned downhill towards the station.

It was icy, there were few people about, which made it all seem like a dream and I felt half sure that if I went back to the house the Old Woman would still be there, with her dogs snuffling round her skirts and a calendar on her lap, working out her plans for the coming summer, and without even thinking, instead of taking the road to the station, I found myself moving at a trot towards the house. But it was in darkness and everything was locked and bolted. I felt like Emily after the death of the Dragon. I could have got in quite easily by poking in one of the cardboard panels in the window, but there was no point. I stood back to take my last look at the house. It was in a bad way. With the broken windows, crumbling brickwork and peeling paint it reminded me of the Old Woman.

I had an hour to spare before my train, and went into the station buffet and bought myself a cup of tea and a huge slice of cake without even counting the cost. I suppose that's how you did things when you had a hundred pounds in your handbag. I was getting expensive tastes. At this rate the hundred pounds wouldn't be there long.

I was munching the cake and feeling quite content really,

when the London train pulled up and I saw a familiar figure get off. I rushed out to have a closer look: it was old Stanley.

'Who's dead now?' I asked.

'Ah,' he said, 'I was hoping I'd find you. Strange finding you right here on the platform, as if it was all arranged.'

I didn't know what he was talking about.

'It occurred to me on the train back to London, which is why I got off at the next station and came right back. Are you fixed up at all?'

'What do you mean?'

'Are you going anywhere from here?'

'What do you think I'd be doing here if I wasn't?'

'Oh, so you are fixed up.'

'I don't know what you mean.'

'Well you see, ever since my wife died . . . '

'Whose wife?'

'My wife.'

'I never knew you were married.'

'Oh yes, I was, for a long time, in fact right up to my bereavement. It's three years now, almost to the day. Sixteenth of January. It's a busy month for funerals, January. The weather I suppose. People like to hang on for Christmas, but once it's over they give up the ghost, though more often than not it's Christmas that does it for them. Haven't had a January yet when I haven't had a funeral, and sometimes I get as many as a dozen. Now take last week . . . '

I waited for him patiently to get to the point, and by the time he got to it I missed my train, and even then he mightn't have got to it at all if I hadn't cut in and asked him what exactly he was trying to tell me.

'Well, it's like this. I'm all on my own you see and I thought I'd get used to it after a while, but I didn't, or at least I haven't done so far, and in fact it gets worse the more it goes on. Don't like it at all, being on my own. I suppose it's different if you've never been married in the first place, but I was, you see, right up to the time of my bereavement. It's three years now, almost to the day – sixteenth of January. A busy month . . . '

175

'Look,' I said, 'are you asking me to come home with you?'
He seemed startled at that.

'No, no, no, I'd never put it like that.'

'Do you want me to be your house-keeper then?'

'My goodness me, no.'

'Your companion?'

'Well yes, in a manner of speaking.'

'What manner of speaking?'

He hesitated for a moment, as if searching for words, then he said: 'Remember some years ago you asked me about opening a launderette?'

'Yes.'

'And I said it was a good idea, but that you'd need a partner who's handy with machines. Well as a matter of fact, I am rather handy with machines and as I'm due to retire, I was wondering if we could perhaps set up together.'

Which we did, in more ways than one, and lived happily ever after, or as near to ever after as counts.